'You don't keep your word, do you, Gil?' she demanded.

'You said—you said you wouldn't touch me unless I invited you to.'

'Ah, but you did,' he said. 'You touched *me* first, remember? That was an invitation if ever I saw one, or so I interpreted it. It isn't always what women say, Cordelia. It's their eyes, their bodies. Yours were begging me to get on with it! You're either a tease, or a virgin, or both!'

Dear Reader

Wouldn't it be wonderful to drop everything and jet off to Australia—the land of surf, sunshine, 'barbies' and, of course, the vast, untamed Outback? Mills & Boon contemporary romances offer you that very chance! Tender and exciting love stories by favourite Australian authors bring vividly to life the city, beach and bush, and introduce you to the most gorgeous heroes that Down Under has to offer...check out your local shops, or with our Readers' Service, for a trip of a lifetime!

The Editor

Lee Stafford was born and educated in Sheffield where she worked as a secretary, and later as a public relations assistant. However, she has been a compulsive scribbler for as long as she can remember. She lives in Sussex with her husband, their two teenage daughters and three cats. To keep fit, she swims and does a weekly dance-exercise class. When not travelling to research new backgrounds, she likes to relax at the small apartment they recently bought in France.

Recent titles by the same author:

SHADOW IN THE WINGS
SUMMER'S ECHO

A HEART DIVIDED

BY

LEE STAFFORD

MILLS & BOON LIMITED
ETON HOUSE   18-24 PARADISE ROAD
RICHMOND   SURREY   TW9 1SR

*First published in Great Britain 1992
by Mills & Boon Limited*

© Lee Stafford 1992

*Australian copyright 1992
Philippine copyright 1992
This edition 1992*

ISBN 0 263 77554 2

*Set in Times Roman 10 on 11¼ pt.
93-9206-57920 C*

Made and printed in Great Britain

CHAPTER ONE

CORDELIA breathed more easily once she was out of the bar of the *fonda*, but the respite was only temporary; she set off up the hill at a cracking pace, forgetting or disregarding the sudden, steep change in altitude, and very soon her sides were aching.

Looking back, she saw that she had left the main road through the village—the only true road, for the rest were all stony, winding tracks—some way below, so that she was gazing down on the crazy, haphazard patterns of roof tiles and white walls, blinding under the high mid-afternoon sun. All around her, closing in the narrow valley on both sides, repelling and shutting out invaders, the mountains towered, abrupt and dramatic, their lower flanks thickly covered by trees, the sharp grey peaks cleaving the intense blue of the sky. Cordelia shuddered involuntarily. She could not help feeling that her presence here was resented.

Turning, she continued to climb, escaping at last from the scrutiny of watchful, suspicious eyes. Civilisation—such as it was, her city-bred mind thought grimly—appeared to peter out here, but then, rounding a final twist in the track, she halted, her breath caught in sudden, unexpected ravishment.

There was, after all, one more house, but such a house that it filled her artist's soul with pure, aesthetic, visual joy, in spite of the fact that she was tired, nervous, and totally unsure of how to proceed with her unlikely mission. She forgot her apprehension in that moment,

5

wishing only that she had her sketchbook and pencils
with her, to capture this idyllic corner.

The house was low, and not very big; one shoulder
of it seemed hunched right into the protective side of
the mountain. The encroaching green of the forest all
but enveloped it, red tiles and chimney peeping out from
beneath the branches. The windows were tiny and multi-
paned, the door half hidden and secretive. What she
could see of the walls was white, but this was very little,
for they were smothered in foliage—profuse climbing
roses and hydrangeas, dark green ivy and blood-scarlet
pelargoniums growing thickly from every crevice, leaving
scarcely an inch bare. Along the first floor, below a
deeply overhanging roof, ran...you could not call it
anything so southerly as a balcony...it was more of a
gallery, veiled by trailing plants which rendered the upper
windows invisible from where she stood.

'Perfect!' she breathed softly. 'It's pure Hänsel and
Gretel...totally enchanted...'

Lacking her sketchpad, she did have her faithful
Pentax along, and she whipped it out to record the scene
and help her, she hoped, to sketch later from memory.
Two half open iron gates led into the small garden, and
Cordelia stepped right up to them, inadvertently rattling
them slightly as she leaned over, angling the lens to get
the full picture.

Frowning into the aperture, she somehow failed to see
the large black and brown German Shepherd dog come
padding softly round the back of the house, ears bristling
warningly. It was the low growl, deep in the animal's
throat, which alerted her, and she looked down, startled,
into the menacing snarl of a set of large white canines,
threateningly bared.

Cordelia knew nothing at all about dogs, and had
never kept one, living as she did in the flat above her
shop, but this creature looked distinctly unfriendly. She

froze, hands still gripped around her camera. Hadn't she read somewhere that animals could smell fear? If so, this one's nose must be having a field day, as horrified thoughts of rabies chased through her head.

'Good dog...good boy...' she said placatingly, and not at all convincingly, and was rewarded by a loud, discouraging bark. She stepped back involuntarily, and the dog responded by bounding forward, barking loudly and threateningly, making it clear that she would be unwise to move. She wasn't about to argue.

'Help!' she called out sharply. 'Will someone please call off this wretched dog?' No one would understand her, of course, but if anyone were home...and she prayed that they were...the sound of her voice, sharp with apprehension, would perhaps elicit a response.

The man who emerged from the house had to stoop slightly to negotiate the low doorway—that was the first thing Cordelia noted. The second was that he possessed the darkest, flintiest eyes she had ever encountered, not melting, as dark eyes often are, but sharp as polished jet. His forehead was compressed into a frown every bit as unwelcoming as the dog's bark; in fact, he looked equally unfriendly.

She had shouted for aid instinctively, in English—not that she spoke more than a few words of Spanish, and certainly none that could cope with this situation. But it astounded her when he addressed her cuttingly in the same language.

'There's no need to carry on so hysterically,' he said, in a tone of withering contempt. 'He's not about to eat you. Here, Pelayo...*aqui*!'

At the command, the dog slunk obediently back to his side, and Cordelia was able to relax a little. But the release of tension had unleashed a touch of indignant anger.

'He wouldn't need to *eat* me, exactly, would he?' she demanded tartly. 'A bite would do. How do I know he's not rabid?'

'That's a typically English prejudice,' the man said loftily. 'He's vaccinated regularly to ensure he does not have rabies, which is more than can be said for dogs in England. Furthermore, any stranger can pass that gate in relative safety. He won't trouble anyone unless he catches them encroaching on his territory.'

His cold, accusing dark glare lighted on the camera in her hand.

'I'm not on the list of tourist attractions,' he pointed out. 'Did I give you permission to photograph my home?'

It was on the edge of Cordelia's tongue to retort that she was scarcely harming the structure of the building by doing so, when all at once, snippets of information and intelligence began to click together in her mind. Here she was, on a hillside on the outskirts of a remote village in Asturias, conducting an argument with a strange man, but in plain English.

Should that not tell her something? There could not be so many people hereabouts who could do that, so perhaps it should be telling her that her search ended here, that this was the man she had been trying to find.

She almost groaned, for she could hardly have made his acquaintance in less auspicious circumstances! Still, it did not really matter what he thought of her personally. She was only the messenger. It was the news she carried which was important.

Shrugging, she slipped her camera back into its case.

'OK, I won't photograph if you object,' she said, with a smile which was meant to be disarming, but which had as much effect as water flung at granite. 'Actually, I think you must be the person I'm looking for,' she pressed on, regardless. 'I mean, it's too much of a coincidence.

You're English, aren't you...and are you, by any chance, Gillan de Mornington?'

His face was without reaction, totally as stone. Cordelia gulped, knocked sideways by his complete and unexpected unresponsiveness.

'No,' he said flatly, 'I'm Gil Montero.' His eyes raked over her, knowledgeably, drawing their own conclusions from her appearance—the halter-necked summer dress she had put on that morning in her hotel room in Castro Urdiales, the soft cream kid sandals, the Pentax in its leather case, and the red hair swept on top of her head, secured with a Paisley-print barrette.

'If you're here to climb mountains, *señorita*, then I'm your man. Otherwise——' and doubt was clearly implicit in his voice '—otherwise, I don't think I can be of any service to you.'

Naturally, it had not occurred to Cordelia at the outset that she would be the one to tell Gillan de Mornington that his father's demise had made him Lord de Mornington, heir to a large estate in Herefordshire and a nine-hundred-year-old title, along with a number of other financial holdings calculated to leave him comfortably rich. She had merely gone along for the ride, so to speak. Now she wished aggrievedly that Bryce Penfold had never suggested she accompany him on this ill-starred trip to Spain.

Bryce was a partner in the legal firm which had looked after her father's affairs. He had dealt with the transfer to Cordelia, after her father's death, of the artists' materials shop and small gallery of local work they had run together in the city of Hereford, a stone's throw from its historic cathedral heart.

Ten years her senior, he had known Cordelia for some years, well enough to offer her a sympathetic shoulder when he found her crying in the studio at the back of the shop, in the middle of a bright summer afternoon.

Cordelia and Denton Harris had been more like friends than father and daughter, and the loss had hit her hard. Not only the actual bereavement, but the months of his illness which preceded it, the visits to the hospital, the many times he had been exhausted from pain, drugs or the side effects of chemotherapy, and the physical toll of caring for him as well as looking after the business. In effect, she had been running it single-handedly for some time.

'You need a break,' Bryce had said. 'Get away from all this for a while. I've got to take a trip to Spain next month—business. Care to come along?'

She had been doubtful. She thought of him as a good friend and adviser, no more, but she was aware that he admired her on a deeper level. There was no room in her heart right now for feelings of that kind, and she could not risk encouraging him to believe that there could be.

He seemed to sense the cause of her hesitation.

'No strings,' he promised. 'I'd like the strings, of course, but never mind. Separate rooms, and all that. It would be good for the painting, don't you think? Bring the old sketchpad along.'

'The painting has been on the back burner for some time,' Cordelia confessed ruefully. 'I don't think I've had a brush in my hand this year.'

'That's understandable. You haven't had a lot of time for yourself,' he agreed cautiously.

Indeed she had not. But there was more to it than that. Painting had always been her first love, the shop a means to support herself. Every spare hour her easel had been up, or she would be out and around, sketching, working towards the glorious 'one day' when she would sell, exhibit, *be* an artist. No longer. Since her father's illness, something had died in her, or at least fallen deeply asleep. She did not seem to have the ability, or even the spark. Only the fugitive need still nagged frustratingly at her, and that, on its own, was useless.

Perhaps Spain would set the creative sap flowing again? It was a totally unknown land to her, a place the very name of which hinted at magic and mystery.

'But I'd have to close the shop,' she said dubiously.

'Close it, then,' Bryce had urged. 'A couple of weeks won't lose you that much custom. You're well enough established in the city. And you're not much use to the business in this state, are you?'

That was undeniably true, and it would be good to get away from this place which she loved, but which, right now, was haunted by painful memories. Her decision was made impulsively, that very day. She would go.

In the short time before they left, Bryce told her a little of the case which had made his journey necessary. It involved the estate of Lord de Mornington, who had died suddenly and unexpectedly, in the prime of life and perfect health, when his hunter took a fence badly, breaking His Lordship's neck.

Cordelia did not move in the same social circles as the de Morningtons, who had owned their Herefordshire acres for longer than anyone cared to work out—in fact, the original bearer of the title had been a Norman knight, one of William the Conqueror's adventurous mercenaries. But she had read of his accident in the local paper, and winced with sympathy. Giles de Mornington had left a widow, a son of twenty-two—Cordelia's own age—and a daughter a few years younger.

'Someone else who has lost a father,' she said. 'I can feel for them. But the family live here, don't they? Why should you have to go to Spain?'

Bryce smiled thinly.

'Lord de Mornington's death has opened up a Pandora's box,' he said. 'His son, Ranulf, is *not* his heir. His father kept this quiet, even from his present family, but he was previously married, when very young, to a Spanish lady. There was a son of that marriage. It didn't work out, she and the boy went back to Spain, where she died a few years later, and he remarried. This son, who must now be in his early thirties, is the new Lord de Mornington.'

Cordelia whistled softly.

'What a story—it can't be for real? It sounds more like a television mini-series, starring Joan Collins!' she smiled, with a spark of amusement rare in her these days. 'But can't you write to this ... whatever his name is?'

'Gillan—it's an old family name. And I already have written to the only address I could locate for him, several times, without receiving a reply.'

'Then surely it's his loss?' Cordelia shrugged. 'Isn't that what happens if the person who stands to benefit can't be traced? The title and estate must devolve on ... Ranulf? What weird names they go in for—are they all throwbacks to their Norman ancestry?'

'Not all. Some are Welsh,' Bryce informed her with a smile. 'Apparently, during the Middle Ages, one of the de Morningtons married the daughter of a Welsh princeling, and started a tradition of intermarriage across the border. As to the inheritance, it's not so simple. Reading between the lines of the papers in my possession, the young Giles De Mornington married his Spanish bride in the face of strong family opposition— they had other plans for him. He never brought her home to Hereford—they lived in Oxford where he was a student—and the family hush-hushed the connection. Perhaps they hoped it wouldn't last. However, this is a very ancient title, subject to archaic conditions, and it can only be passed on through the male line, from eldest son to eldest son.'

'That must have been a considerable blow to Ranulf,' Cordelia mused, 'particularly since he didn't even know he had a half-Spanish elder brother.'

'Half-brother,' Bryce corrected pedantically. 'But you're right, Ranulf may not like it—indeed, his father may not have liked it, for all I know. I don't suppose he expected to die for some considerable time, but he certainly left a hornets' nest behind by not telling anyone! However, this chap in Spain is the sole legal heir. I need to find him, if he's alive, which one presumes he must be. Lady de Mornington prefers that I handle this discreetly, myself, rather than through lawyers over there. So to Spain I must go, Cordelia. Are you with me?'

'How could I refuse? It all sounds fascinating,' she said, the first sparkle of interest since her father's death gleaming in the intensely blue eyes.

They sailed from Plymouth on the car ferry to Santander. The woman Giles de Mornington had married did not hail from the sunny Mediterranean *costas* familiar to British tourists, but from the remote, little-known, mountainous region of Asturias, which stretched inland from the Atlantic Ocean. It was not a good beginning. The sea was rough in the Bay of Biscay, both Bryce and Cordelia suffered from seasickness, and were still slightly green as they drove off the ship.

The only address they had for the new Lord de Mornington was a hotel in the coastal resort of Castro Urdiales, approximately seventy kilometres east of Santander.

'It's a very old address, and was difficult to trace, so it may not prove much more than a starting point,' Bryce warned her pessimistically. But Cordelia's spirits were revived by the beautiful coastal scenery, the succession of aquamarine bays with green, white-frothed breakers rolling on to cliff-girt beaches, and the good coast road connecting the small, pretty resorts along the Cantabrian shore. She hoped there would be an opportunity for her to explore this lovely area, in addition to delivering the news of his inheritance to Gillan de Mornington.

Castro Urdiales, where they arrived in the afternoon, after a leisurely drive and a protracted stop for lunch, was an attractive and appealing place, part holiday resort, part fishing port. The older quarter, surrounding the picturesque harbour, was overlooked by a large Gothic church and the remains of a once impressive Templar castle. There was a beach and a tree-shaded promenade lined with hotels old enough to give it an air of well-established respectability—a solid town, not a fly-by-night tourist emporium.

'Nice,' Cordelia commented, her eyes assessing the pictorial qualities of the colourful harbour dominated by the grey stone of the castle. 'I don't blame His future Lordship for settling here, but I wonder what he does for a living. If his permanent address is a hotel, perhaps he runs it?'

'I doubt it.' Bryce drove slowly along the main thoroughfare, dodging jay-walkers, his eyes scanning the street for their destination. 'It's called the Hostal de la Costa, and its proprietress is a Señora Merche Ramirez. It took a lot of investigation to track our mysterious heir this far, and I'm not too sanguine about the likelihood of finding him here.'

Finding the hotel itself was not that simple either, but finally they located it, on a side street, at a point where the newer area merged into the fishermen's quarters. An old building, with a covered arcade at ground level, and partially glassed-in balconies above, evidence that the weather along this coast was not always as benign as it appeared today.

Reception was staffed by a handsome, elegant woman, perhaps in her late thirties, the proprietress herself, as she admitted when Bryce asked politely, 'Señora Ramirez?'

Their queries were fraught with difficulty. She spoke fractured English and a little French, and neither of them had more than a few words of Spanish. At first she seemed puzzled when Bryce said he was looking for Gillan de Mornington, then her face cleared, and clouded again. She leaned her long, eloquent torso over the reception desk, chin in hand, fingers teasing the ends of dark auburn hair, artfully streaked with shades of paprika, and said knowingly, as the penny dropped, 'Ah! You look for the English *señor*, Gil—*si*? What he has done now?'

Cordelia glanced quickly at Bryce, who was doing his best to look blandly non-committal—difficult even for him, in view of her reaction.

'Done? Why, nothing, to my knowledge, *señora—nada*,' he assured her. 'I am a lawyer—*abogado*. I have some family news for him.'

Merche Ramirez frowned.

'*Lo siento, señor*. I cannot help you,' she said, with an expressive shrug. 'He is not here. I do not see him these...' she counted swiftly '...three years, maybe more.'

So, as Bryce had feared all along, it was not going to be so easy, Cordelia reflected.

'Do you ... perhaps ... know where we can find him?' she asked slowly.

Señora Ramirez surveyed her carefully and with a great deal of thought, almost as if she were considering exposing Cordelia to the possibility of great danger, or untold delights, neither of which prospects appealed to her. Then she looked at Bryce, in the smooth English security of his well-tailored trousers and jacket, his short,

neat hair and professional calm, and decided that
perhaps it might be risked.

'I hear...not long ago...he is in a village...La Vega.
It is in the Picos de Europa—the mountains,' she offered.

Bryce sighed.

'*Perdóneme, señora...*' He turned to Cordelia. 'It
looks as if we must venture into the mountains in search
of our hero, but after that crossing, I don't fancy setting
off right now,' he said. 'What do you say we stay here
tonight, consult the map, and make an early start in the
morning?'

'I think it's the best idea you've had all day,' she agreed
fervently. 'I'm for a good dinner, and a night in a bed
that *isn't* pitching about!'

Señora Ramirez had two rooms available, so they
checked in. Bryce gave Cordelia first choice, and she
plumped for the one at the front, because it had a little
balcony from where she could just see the comings and
goings of the boats in the harbour. Dinner, they learned
with some horror, would not be served before nine-
thirty—this was usual for Spain, where everything in the
evening was geared to a much later start. But there were
plenty of bars open serving *tapas*—bits and pieces of
interesting seafood, cooked meat and salad—and they
strolled about, picking and choosing.

'You know,' said Bryce, 'this could be fun if it weren't
for the elusive aristocrat. We could make the most of
our time here together, Cordelia. I hardly ever see you
in Hereford.'

A couple of drinks must have relaxed his good intentions. He reached out and took her hand, drawing her
closer, and she snatched it away again, jumping back.

'Bryce! You promised—no strings!'

'So I did, I know,' he groaned. 'But it isn't easy, in
this romantic place, especially when you're looking so
confoundedly pretty!'

A slight embarrassment hung over them as they ate dinner at the Hostal de la Costa. Could one, after all, go away with a man and expect things to remain platonic? Cordelia wondered ruefully. The year behind her, with her father's illness and death, her constant preoccupation with the business, had not been easy. Romance had been the last thing on her mind, and still was. Her raw emotions had yet to recover from the pain of losing a loved one, the shop still needed to make enough profit to support her, which was by no means certain. And at the back of her mind, always nagging away, for all she tried to silence it, was the worry and doubt about the creative impulse which seemed to have deserted her. Would she ever paint again?

And now here was Bryce, coming on all sentimental, and they still had who knew how many miles to travel together! Perhaps Spain had not been such a good idea after all?

Cordelia's balcony faced a café across the street, and while it was fun to sit a while after retiring, watching life flow around its pavement tables, it was less pleasant to find that same life going on, far into the early hours, after she had gone to bed. At last, somewhere around two-thirty a.m. quiet fell, but after only a few short hours another kind of racket began, as the fishermen returned to the harbour and set about unloading their catch, heaving crates of fish and conversing loudly among themselves. Why did everyone in Spain have to shout so? she wondered ungraciously, diving back under the covers and trying to get back to sleep.

When she did finally give up the fight and decide she might as well get up, since they had planned an early start, it was to find that Bryce had been stricken by some bug.

He tottered downstairs looking greener than he had when they drove off the ferry, and distinctly shaky.

'It's no use—I can't travel today. I should never have tried to get out of bed, and I intend going straight back,' he announced querulously. 'I shouldn't have eaten those *tapas* either. I'd forgotten that seafood never agrees with me.'

'Oh, dear!' Cordelia said sympathetically. 'Is there anything I can do?'

'Not a thing. I don't want to see a soul for the rest of the day!' he declared. 'You'll have to look after yourself, Cordelia—spend the day on the beach or something. Perhaps I'll feel better tomorrow, although right now I can't imagine that I ever shall!'

Sorry for him as she was, Cordelia could not help thinking treacherously that he was being a bit of an old woman about it! Neither was she too entranced by the notion of lying on a beach alone. Although this was her first visit to Spain, she had heard enough about the kind of attentions a lone English girl could expect to attract. Bryce's tentative romantic overtures had been one thing, a day discouraging the local Casanovas was quite another.

'That would be a waste of a day,' she said. 'If you're sure you don't need me, why don't I check out this La Vega place, see if Gillan de Mornington is there, and deliver the papers to him? It would give me something to do, and I'd like to help.'

He was doubtful.

'On your own? Oh, I don't know about that, Cordelia. Would it be safe?'

That decided her. 'Don't be silly,' she said, annoyed by his assumption of her maidenly fragility. 'This is Spain, not the African bush, and we aren't in the Middle Ages! I live alone, I run a business alone. I'm a perfectly competent driver, and I won't wreck your car. *Of course* I'll be all right. You go back to bed and rest. And don't worry!'

Although she could see he was not happy about it, he was not really in any condition to argue with her, and in the end, meekly did as he was told. Cordelia saw him settled, explained to Señora Ramirez that Señor Penfold was not well, and asked if she would kindly keep an eye on him.

'*Cierto*—my pleasure.' Merche Ramirez eyed Cordelia curiously. 'You go somewhere, *señorita*?'

'I'm going to La Vega, to see if I can find Mr de Mornington,' she replied briskly.

The Spanish woman's eyes widened with something like alarm.

'*Señorita*, you very young, and *muy bonita*,' she said urgently. 'Señor Gil, he is...' she struggled to find the correct words in English '...he likes women, many women, but he is not good man for them. Take much care!'

Cordelia met her eyes and saw two very different emotions in conflict on her face. One was genuine concern, a warning sincerely meant. The other was harder to identify, but it looked oddly like jealousy. 'You *muy bonita*'...Merche Ramirez did not *want* her to meet Gillan de Mornington.

At some point in the past, Cordelia realised with a shock, perhaps several years ago, when he had lived here, these two had had a relationship. From the intensity of this woman's reactions, Cordelia was sure it had been passionate. She concluded it had ended badly. Presumably he had left her, and Merche was trying to tell her that the man she was seeking had that kind of reputation where women were concerned.

So Gillan de Mornington was what in earlier times might have been called a rake? A true son of the English landed gentry, Cordelia thought with an amused if disparaging sniff, enjoying his pleasures abroad as such gentlemen had done for centuries? So what? It had nothing to do with her. She was only going to deliver her news and return to Castro Urdiales. He would hardly have time to seduce her, even if she had been of a mind to be seduced. Which she most definitely was not. Her curiosity was whetted, but that was all.

'*Gracias, señora*, but this is only business,' she explained reassuringly. 'There's no need for you to worry about me.'

She was to remember those words ruefully, many times in the future, wondering how she could have set off with such insouciance, blindly convinced of her own immunity.

But when she gave that assurance, she had yet to meet the man she still thought of, then, as Gillan de Mornington. How could she have known what, or whom, she would find, and how that meeting would overturn her life?

Perhaps the land should have warned her. This was not a gentle, meandering drive into gradually rising hills, the altitude increasing step by step. The roads, once she turned inland at San Vicente de la Barquera, were alarming; hairpin bends hugging deep drops, often untroubled by crash barriers, had her gripping the steering wheel until her wrists ached and her knuckles whitened.

One minute, it seemed, the Picos were nowhere in sight, and then suddenly, dramatically, she was among them. The road threaded tortuously through breathtaking, rocky defiles, alongside rushing torrents, then climbing, climbing, until all was rock and scree and wild grey peaks, under a savage blue sky. The villages were like tiny oases, outposts in this mountain wilderness, the road a thin lifeline, barely stringing them together.

Perspiration broke out on Cordelia's brow. She felt more lonely here than ever in her life, alone and yet shut in, sealed off from the world beyond. Threatened and oppressed. How could an Englishman, the product of a gentler landscape, choose to live here?

And then she came to La Vega, a scattering of white, red-tiled houses where the valley widened marginally, just enough to allow for civilisation, a village shop or two, a couple of bars, one simple *fonda*, or inn, which seemed to be full of men. Old men sitting inside, playing cards, young men at the outside tables, legs sprawled, looking macho and watching her with scarcely veiled interest as she parked the car and forced herself to walk in.

With her minimal Spanish, she asked the man behind the bar if anyone knew the whereabouts of Gillan de Mornington. It somehow did not surprise her when no one would admit that they did.

She thought it must be a male conspiracy, and her face reddened with embarrassment as it occurred to her that perhaps they thought she was one of his cast-off lovers, and were covering his tracks. Closing ranks against a female intruder who threatened to spoil his fun. Merche Ramirez had, after all, as good as intimated that he was that sort of man.

Cordelia could only retreat from the watching eyes with their half-closed stares and stonily polite head-shakes, and suddenly she thought that maybe Bryce's irritating caution had not been misplaced, and it had been a kind of madness for her to come here, looking for a man she did not know, of whom what little she had learned indicated that it would not be a good thing for her to make his acquaintance.

For this was not the Spain she had left behind her on the coast. That, unknown to her though it was, had enough points of reference, enough similarity to the world she knew, for her to cope with it. This was a different land, an older society, almost another age, which surrounded her. She could sense the difference in the air, and knew that it was she who was the alien here.

Go away, it seemed to be telling her, you're not wanted, and it would have required little more urging for her to get back into Bryce's car, turn around, and return the way she had come.

But Cordelia, for all the delicate fragility of her appearance, was made of stronger stuff, so she did no such thing. She squared her slender shoulders, and in her totally unsuitable sandals, trudged off up the hill towards her personal encounter with destiny.

CHAPTER TWO

THE man who had introduced himself to her as Gil
Montero but who *had*, she reasoned, to be Gillan de
Mornington, was a strange mixture of his parents'
nationalities. It wasn't so much that he had the char-
acteristics of both—his eyes were very dark, but his hair
was a shade of dark brown, tinged with chestnut, that
you could see on any English street. It was more than
that . . . his face changed with his expression, chameleon-
like, looking at one moment very English, and then the
next, the Spaniard in him took over completely.

She tried a polite smile.

'Can we establish one simple fact?' she asked coolly.
'Whatever you happen to call yourself right now, you
are Gillan de Mornington, are you not?'

The anger on the lean face was all the more frightening because of its coldness, a deadly accuracy which
focused on her as its sole and quite legitimate target.

'I've always called myself Gil Montero, and I see no
reason to change that now,' he said icily. 'Montero was
my mother's name, and I'm proud of it. As for the
other—yes, I will admit that I have the right to use it,
if I choose to. Which I don't.'

He shifted position easily, the big dog sinking on to
its haunches at his side. He was not a large man in the
sense of bulk, but he looked incredibly fit and tough,
the muscles beneath the well-worn denims and cotton
shirt would be as strong, she guessed, as ropes of iron.
She had somehow expected a playboy ladies' man—the

only hint of it was the long, curving, strangely sensuous mouth beneath the straight, firm nose.

'You now know who I am, and that this house belongs to me,' he went on, just a glimmer of humour visible beneath his cold manner. 'That gives you a distinct advantage, since I haven't a clue who you are, or why you're here. Would it be too much to ask you to enlighten me a little?'

'I'm Cordelia Harris.' In spite of his faint sarcasm, it seemed the polite thing to do to extend her hand, and after a moment's hesitation, he took it. His grip was hard, his skin bronzed—an outdoor man, but with something contemplative about his eyes. 'My name won't mean anything to you, of course, but I'm here on behalf of Faulkner and Penfold, who are a firm of solicitors in Hereford.'

She saw his eyes narrow infinitesimally, and quailed suddenly as the full import of what she had to tell him hit her. She had never before had to impart the news of someone's death—why had the seriousness of this not occurred to her when she blithely undertook to come here? She remembered the quiet sympathy of the hospital sister who had given *her* the sad news of her father's death. It could not have been done more kindly, but had that really helped? Could anything?

'There's no easy way to say this.' She launched herself bluntly into the necessity. 'I'll come straight to the point. Your father, Lord de Mornington, died recently. I'm very sorry.'

His face remained totally closed and expressionless.

'You're sorry? There's no need for you to express any sympathy for me,' he said harshly. 'If you're expecting me to be moved, I'll have to disappoint you. I haven't seen or heard from my father since I was five, and I can scarcely remember him. It wasn't really worth your while

coming all this way to tell me that, but thank you, anyhow, for your trouble.'

She sensed that she was being dismissed, and that any
moment now he would turn and disappear back into the
house, the dog at his side.

'But that's not the whole of it!' she cried. 'What I
have to tell you is that you are his legal heir. *You* are
now Lord de Mornington.'

Gil Montero looked at her, briefly, with a kind of incredulous amusement which he seemed to be trying hard
to smother. He failed, and leaning on the gate, succumbed to laughter so explosive that it almost brought
tears to his eyes.

Cordelia watched him, astonished and outraged, for
no one—*no one*—should receive the news of another's
death this way. How could he be so heartless, so...so
unfeeling?

At last he straightened up, got his humour under
control, although she could still discern a furtive gleam
of laughter hovering in his eyes, a slight twitch at the
corners of the incongruously sensitive mouth.

'Have you quite finished?' she asked frostily.

'Oh, yes—quite.' Was there mockery in his voice, and
was it directed at her, because she found his amusement
misplaced? He said, 'Look, don't get me wrong. I wasn't
laughing because you told me he was dead. I did hear
somewhere along the line that he'd remarried and had
a family, and they have my sincere sympathy in their
loss. But that's just it—it *is* their loss, not mine. Truly,
I can't be so hypocritical as to pretend to grieve for a
man I never really knew, who abandoned me as a child.
And the idea of *me* as Lord de Mornington is ludicrous
beyond belief. Tell them to pass the title to someone else,
whoever's next in line. Presumably his second wife has
a son?'

'She has. But he can't inherit,' Cordelia told him. 'There's some kind of entail or something on the property, which means it has to be passed from eldest son to eldest son. It has to come to you.'

A moment ago he had appeared as English as she. Now she saw again that austere Spanish face, eyelids veiling whatever emotions he might be feeling, lips drawn tightly together. It occurred to her fleetingly that her news might have affected him more deeply than he was prepared to admit. He was silent for a long minute, and respecting his silence, she remained quiet too.

Then he sighed and said resignedly, 'You'd better come in and sit down. It's remiss of me to keep you standing out here in the sun.'

He opened the gate wider to admit her, and seeing her glance nervously at the dog, said, 'Don't worry about Pelayo. If I ask you in, he presumes you're all right. He trusts my judgement.'

'*What* do you call him? Pel...?'

'Pelayo. The original was the Christian general who defeated the Moors in 722 at Covadonga, which is just up the road from here, so to speak. A noble name for a noble animal.'

Affection was evident in his tone, but there must still have been some doubt left on her face, for he said, with obvious amazement, 'You don't like dogs?'

'I wouldn't say that, exactly. I've never had much to do with them. I live in a flat in Hereford, where it wouldn't be fair to keep one.'

To prove her point, Cordelia reached out tentatively and stroked the warm brown fur as she followed Gil Montero down the path and into the Hänsel and Gretel house, and since the dog did not object, she presumed that, as his owner had said, he had accepted her presence.

The thick stone walls made it blessedly cool inside the house, but there was a large fireplace, and Cordelia thought the same walls would ensure warmth in the winter, when surely these mountains would have snow. The stone-flagged floor was partly covered by colourful woven rugs, the furniture was dark and rustic. Sunlight filtered in through windows at either end of the room, picking up the warm red of a coverlet thrown over a couch, flowers in an earthenware vase, blue and white pottery on an old dresser.

There was a large table strewn with open books, maps and papers. Some kind of work had obviously been in progress, which her arrival had interrupted. Gil Montero pulled out a chair for her, fetched a carafe of wine and poured her a glass, as if suddenly remembering the long Spanish tradition of hospitality.

At the other end of the room, through an open door, Cordelia could see a kitchen garden planted with lettuces, cabbages, beans, among a profusion of flowers. There were chickens in a pen, scratching happily at the earth, and on the path a tabby cat was enthusiastically washing a brood of kittens. Everything pointed to a settled, if not to say permanent existence of some duration. Was this the footloose philanderer Merche Ramirez had warned her to avoid?

Even as she was puzzling over him, she caught him looking at her with curious disbelief.

'Excuse my staring,' he said, 'but I find it difficult to take you at face value. Somehow, you don't look like a solicitor.'

'Gracious, I'm not!' she said quickly, realising that this must have been a false impression she had given. 'In fact, I'm not here in any official capacity at all. I'm simply a friend of Bryce Penfold, one of the partners. Unfortunately, Bryce didn't feel well this morning, so I volunteered to deliver the papers to you on his behalf.'

Delving into her capacious handbag, she took out the long manila envelope she had been guarding carefully all day, and handed it to him. He simply tossed it on to the table, unopened.

'So where is Señor Penfold now, while you're doing his work for him?' he demanded.

'I told you, he's not well, or he would have come himself. He's . . . he's in the Hostal de la Costa, in Castro Urdiales, where we stayed last night,' Cordelia faltered, taken aback by the abruptness of the question. Didn't he believe anything she had told him? Swiftly, she counter-attacked. 'That was the only address for you that Faulkner and Penfold had been able to trace, and it was Señora Ramirez, whom I believe you know, who directed us here.'

She had expected this to disconcert him, but instead a lazy smile played around that amazing mouth, his eyelids lowering a fraction.

'Ah, yes—Merche,' he said softly, as he might have spoken had that lady stabbed him in the back, but his voice held only faint sorrow, and no venom. And those three words, unadorned, with no explanation, confirmed Cordelia's intuitive suspicion that, once, those two had been far more than friends.

'She did mention that she hadn't seen you for over three years,' Cordelia added, aware that she was probing where really she should not, but unable to resist the temptation to draw him out.

'Has it been that long?' His voice was light and unconcerned. He remembered Merche Ramirez appreciatively, but no more. *Her* memories were more intense, and more bitter. Perhaps, Cordelia thought, as she glanced covertly at that mouth, he *was* just as Merche had said, a sexual dilettante who moved casually from female to female, uncaring.

He refilled his glass, and would have done the same with hers, had she not shaken her head.

'Please...Señor Montero——' she remembered, just in time, to address him as he preferred '—won't you open the envelope? Then perhaps you could talk to Bryce. He will of course want to come and see you himself, just as soon as he feels better.'

He sighed patiently.

'You really don't get the message, do you?' he said. 'I see I shall have to spell it out for you. I'm not remotely interested in the contents of that envelope, or in the de Mornington title and estate. It can be no conceivable concern of mine, you must see that. My life is here, and I'm happy with it *as it is*. Do you understand?'

'No, I don't!' Cordelia exclaimed heatedly. 'I don't even understand what it is that you do here, exactly, which is so wonderful that you can't bear to abandon it!'

His smile was sympathetic.

'You're obviously a city girl, so I don't suppose you can,' he said with faint dismissiveness. 'It's quite simple. I take parties of people walking and climbing in the mountains. I have my house, my animals, the village and the Picos. It may not seem very much to you, but I happen to be perversely devoted to all of them.'

Cordelia, who had just lost the only family she had ever had, and could not see how anyone could pass up the chance of acquiring a new one, almost choked.

'That isn't what I meant. But yes, I can see how you might find this way of life quite pleasant now, while you're young enough to enjoy it. But what then?'

'I'm an Asturian,' he said obstinately. 'I shall be tough as old boots well into old age, and I shall walk these mountains for as long as I can. When I'm finally too decrepit, I shall sit in the *fonda*, drinking cider and playing cards with the other old boys.'

Was he laughing at her? She did not think he could be serious.

'You're an Englishman, Señor Montero—or at least, half of you is. Listen to yourself—you speak English as well as I do.'

'Naturally. I spoke it continuously until I was five. I studied at Cambridge. I've taught English in Spain, and Spanish in England, and I can assure you, I'm equally at home in either language. But by temperament and upbringing, I'm a Spaniard. My mother was born at Cangas de Onis, not twenty miles from here. This is my home. Can I say more?'

He had a valid point, Cordelia was prepared to admit, but he also had a duty, his by birth, to the de Mornington estate, and she did not think he had the right simply to turn his back on it and pretend it did not exist.

'Nevertheless, you can't avoid your responsibilities,' she told him. 'There are matters connected with the estate which only you can decide, things which need your signature, your assent—Bryce will be able to explain all that better than I can. And there's the family, who need to know what you intend to do. You can't keep them hanging on, uncertain—it isn't fair.'

He gave a snort of contemptuous disbelief.

'I was certainly kept hanging on for a fair while, wouldn't you say? Now, all of a sudden, my presence is required. No, I'm not bitter about it—I just don't care. But kindly don't preach to me about responsibilities. Take your envelope back to your friend Mr Penfold, and say thanks—but no, thanks.'

It would have been an easy matter for Cordelia, and she would have been perfectly within her rights, to let it rest there, to go back to Bryce and say she was sorry but she hadn't got anywhere, and it was up to him to take whatever steps he thought necessary.

Why then was she so reluctant to take this simple way out? It wasn't only that there was a stubborn core to her

which refused to accept defeat, although she recognised
this obstinacy—not always a virtue—in herself.

Over and beyond that, this man intrigued and troubled
her. She did not, she told herself, particularly like him.
He had a steely quality which could be almost frightening, and which promised that if you came up against
him, one way or another, you would lose, or be hurt.
But he represented a challenge, and for the first time in
months she was not thinking only of her own sorrow,
but of the unknown de Mornington family, and theirs.
Gil had said he was not bitter about having been deserted by his father as a child, but she thought he was,
even if, perhaps, he did not acknowledge that emotion.

Mornington Hall was part of him, was in his blood,
whether he liked it or not. He had a stepmother, a half-
sister and half-brother whom he did not know, and in
Cordelia's eyes that was sad for all of them.

Whatever it was that motivated her, she knew she could
not give up so easily. But head-on confrontation with
Gil was getting her nowhere, since he was even more
stubborn than she. She would have to be subtler than
that.

'Señor Montero,' she said, employing her most
winning smile, 'You're quite right. It's not my place to
tell you what you should do. I'm only a disinterested
thirty party, an intermediary. However, I've had a long,
hard drive, and I'm tired. I don't fancy driving back to
Castro Urdiales tonight—these roads are bad enough in
daylight! Is there anywhere I can stay?'

He smiled too, an amused respect in his eyes telling
her he was not fooled by her sudden capitulation.

'Bravo, Miss Harris,' he said, almost conversa-
tionally. 'You know, it's a fact that women like you—
slim and petite, who look as if they'd snap in your
hands—generally have wills of iron and cussed natures!
But don't hold your breath—my decision will be the same

in the morning, whatever means you use to try and subvert it.'

No one likes to be seen through, and Cordelia was no exception. The suggestive hint lurking in his last words, especially, had her seething with indignation.

'Don't hold *your* breath, Señor Montero—I wouldn't be that interested in the result, even if the de Morningtons were paying me commission!' she snapped. 'Just to get things straight—I don't like you, I don't like this place, or these dreadful mountains, and I shall be glad to get away from all three! Right now!'

She reached the door, and although she never heard Gil's soft word of command, she found her exit blocked by Pelayo. He didn't bark or growl, he was just *there*, he was very large, and she wasn't one hundred per cent sure he would take kindly to being pushed aside.

'*Please call your dog!*' she said slowly and carefully, from between gritted teeth.

Gil uttered a soft laugh, got up, and came to stand in the doorway at her side. It was a very narrow aperture, and Pelayo took up rather a lot of it, so man and girl were of necessity very close. She didn't care for it. It disturbed her profoundly, for now she was very certain that Merche was right, and this man was dangerous. He probably could snap her in two with his hands, but from the conquering look in his eyes, and his stance, a hand on the wall either side of her head, which brought them no more than a breath apart, she did not think that was what he had in mind. Her heart was pounding, the blood vessels in her head were expanding and contracting rhythmically, and the altitude had nothing to do with either.

'I'm partial to a bit of good old-fashioned dislike, as an aperitif,' he said calmly. 'But don't get too angry, Miss Harris. Anger really turns me on.'

Every warning system her body possessed was screaming red alert, but she had no will, no power to move. His head bent towards hers, he was going to kiss her, and she could do nothing—nothing—to prevent it. Her eyes widened, and her breath was stranded somewhere in her throat.

And then he stepped back, deliberately. Her exit was clear, and she was free to go. So why didn't she?

'Don't worry,' he said mildly, 'I'm not going to suggest you stay here. This is a very small village, and everyone would be talking about it by morning. The *fonda* is simple but clean, and the food is good.'

She said, 'I'm not going to stay at all.'

'I think you must. As you said yourself, these roads are not ideal in darkness for those who are unused to them. You're obviously tired, and it would be very foolish. Come on, I'll introduce you to Luis, who owns the *fonda*. He's perfectly safe—his wife, three children, and his mother-in-law all live on the premises.'

Cordelia had slept very little the previous night, it had been a very long day, and she was utterly depleted, with an exhaustion which was not merely physical. Arguing with this man, simply being in his company, was a hazard she had not allowed for in her calculations. All she wanted was a meal, a hot shower, a bed for the night, and the quickest possible getaway from La Vega tomorrow. There was no need for her to see Gil de Mornington/Montero again, after she checked in at the *fonda*, she reassured herself, as she reluctantly acceded to his urging.

The bar of the *fonda* was still full of men, but what a difference, now, to her reception! Everyone called out *'Olà!'* to Gil and smiled politely at her, several men slapped him on the back, someone bought him a beer, and her a glass of wine, and he seemed to be involved in several running discussions all at the same time. In

Spanish, of course, and she could not deny the truth of his claim to speak the language as easily as he had spoken English to her. These same people who had been reluctant to give her the time of day, earlier, were now all affability, because she was with Gil.

'Luis's wife, Dolores, will show you your room,' he said, tearing himself away from what appeared to be, from the names she had heard bandied around, a discussion of an international football match, televised recently. 'Dinner's at nine—early for Spain, but this is a farming community.'

And he left her, just like that. For a moment, Cordelia stood, bemused, watching him shoulder his way across the bar and out of the room. She had known him for such a very short time, but in it, they had argued deeply, he had puzzled and enraged her, and at the very last almost made a pass at her. Now he walked away from her, totally unconcerned, and she was aware of a strange, altogether irrational sense of loss. Minutes ago, she had thought she would be glad to see the back of him, so this reaction did not make any sense. Sighing, she followed Dolores up the stairs.

Her room was small, sparsely furnished, but spotlessly clean. The *fonda* did not run to anything so grand as en-suite facilities, but there was a shower-room at the end of the corridor. Cordelia showered gratefully. Not knowing how long the journey would take, she had brought only an overnight bag, but the only change of clothes she had were jeans and a sweatshirt, in case the weather turned nasty, so she put on her dress again, for dinner, hoping it still looked clean. Her long hair tended to erupt into a mass of curls when damp, so she fluffed it out with her fingers and left it loose.

Then she stood at her window, watching a spectacular sunset over the mountains. It was beautiful here, undeniably. But it was a fierce, wild beauty which did not appeal to her. All her own landscapes were of the gentle, wooded, undulating Herefordshire countryside, little black and white timbered villages drowning in apple orchards, somnolent trees and venerable bridges reflecting themselves in the broad River Wye. Could she ever paint this savage splendour, even if she wanted to? If the land made the man, Gil Montero and his mountain wilderness were well suited!

It was not until she checked her handbag, before going down to dinner, that Cordelia realised the long manila envelope was not there—that it was, in fact, still on Gil's table, where she had left it.

Had he simply omitted to give it back to her, after making clear his intention to do so? She did not believe a man like that did anything accidentally, so perhaps, despite himself, he was curious. Perhaps, after all, her journey here had not been entirely a failure. Because she had no intention whatsoever of going back to his house to collect the last will and testament of Giles, Lord de Mornington! Of that she was sure beyond the possibility of doubt.

Before going in to dinner, Cordelia made a phone call to Bryce in Castro Urdiales. This was not as easy as it might have appeared. The telephone was in a corner of the noisy bar, where everyone seemed to be talking at once, and yet another football match was in progress on the television. It took her several tries to make the connection, but finally she succeeded and was put through to Bryce's room.

'I suppose I'm feeling a little better,' he told her, in answer to her initial query, 'although I've spent most of the day in bed. Señora Ramirez has looked after me splendidly, running up and down with hot drinks, cold drinks, or simply to see how I am.'

'Perhaps she has a penchant for stray Englishmen,' Cordelia remarked drily. She could not help thinking that he was rather enjoying his temporary invalidism, and having the redoubtable Merche prancing up and downstairs attending to him. But since she had not confided to him Merche's warning about Gil Montero, and he was not the sort of person to have guessed intuitively at the relationship between the two, Bryce seemed puzzled by her comment.

'I haven't the faintest idea what you're talking about. But I did expect you back tonight. What on earth is taking you so long?'

'The roads are awful, Bryce,' she excused herself, 'I daren't risk myself or your car driving them after dark, so I've taken a room at the small hotel here.'

She paused. 'Also, I'm having trouble with our reluctant aristocrat. He doesn't even deign to use the family name, but prefers to call himself Gil Montero. He says he has no interest in the de Mornington inheritance, and no intention of uprooting himself in order to claim it. He simply doesn't want to know.'

Bryce was disbelieving and faintly irritated.

'What nonsense—no one turns his nose up at that much money,' he insisted. 'Doesn't he realise that all else apart, it will make him a rich man as well as a titled one? I should never have let you undertake explaining it to him on your own—you can't have represented the matter accurately. I shall have to talk to him myself.'

'You can try, by all means,' Cordelia almost snapped back, annoyed that he seemed to be hinting that she had not tried sufficiently hard, or had somehow clouded the issue. 'You'll have your work cut out, I can promise you. He understands perfectly, and wants nothing to do with it.'

She replaced the receiver, leaving him still expostulating at the other end. Her voice had been raised, but she was fairly sure that no one in the room would have understood her. She was attracting a fair number of attentive stares, but that, she reasoned, was probably just because she was a lone woman in a room full of men. Looking purposefully straight ahead, she marched out of the bar and headed for the dining-room.

Dolores met her at the door with a smile. The dining-room was not large, and several of its tables were already occupied. The *padrona*, however, knew exactly where she was going to seat Cordelia, and led her directly to a table by the window, whose occupant was already enjoying an *aperitivo*.

His concession to dining out was a clean, slightly newer pair of denims, and a white casual shirt, but as he stood up and pulled out her chair, Cordelia reflected faintly that Gil Montero was not likely to trouble himself about the impression he made on others.

'I didn't think you should dine alone,' he said. Looking her up and down with a close, careful regard which made her tender redhead's skin prickle, he added, 'Might I say that your hair suits you much better, worn loose like that. It's softer, more feminine. Makes you appear more... approachable.'

Cordelia considered the wisdom of slugging him over his arrogant head with the wooden breadbasket on the table, and regretfully decided it would be inadvisable. Who the hell did he think he was, and why should he believe she cared for his opinion?

'I wouldn't have thought looking approachable was a good idea, on the whole, in Spain,' she pronounced loftily. 'I simply left my hair down because it was wet.'

'You're safe enough here,' he said defensively. 'I can assure you you're not in danger of being hassled in a small village like this, where everyone knows everyone else. But the concept of a woman on her own is not appreciated hereabouts. You need to be someone's wife, mother, daughter... or lover, to fit into the general scheme of things.'

'How charmingly old-fashioned,' Cordelia said drily, and he shrugged, untroubled by her sarcasm.

'Maybe, but modernity only skims the surface in most societies. Scratch hard, and you'll unearth something more basic.'

'Are you "basic", Mr Montero?' she queried lightly, and was rewarded by a long, thoughtful scrutiny.

'If you mean where women are concerned, actually, I prefer those who have their own lives and interests,' he said. 'In theory, it should tend to make them less likely to turn possessive on one. In practice, however, one has to admit it's sometimes otherwise.'

'Like Señora Ramirez,' said Cordelia, without thinking, then wished she had bitten her tongue as the flint-dark eyes raked her with questioning. 'As . . . as an example of a woman with her own concern,' she added quickly, but he was not fooled.

'I wonder what Merche has been telling you about me?' he mused, with speculative humour, and Cordelia's translucent skin succumbed to a treacherous blush.

'Nothing, really,' she said quickly, and then, with a surge of recklessness, since it did not matter much what he thought of her, she decided to stir the waters. 'She merely indicated that you're the kind of man nice girls should avoid.'

He laughed with real amusement.

'Oh, dear—poor Merche! The truth is that she and I plugged a gap for each other for a while, no more. I was . . . drifting, and she'd lost her husband a year or so before. Unfortunately, she was trying to find a replacement for him, and common sense should have told a woman of her experience that I wasn't the man for the job. What she told you was quite right, though, and anyhow, I'm not interested in nice girls.'

'Or they in you, perhaps?' Cordelia retorted softly. Conceited beast! she was saying to herself.

'Well, you tell me, Miss Harris.' He grinned and picked up the menu. 'I assume you're a nice girl?'

A stinging retort rose to her lips, which she was obliged to stifle, since Dolores was now hovering by the table, waiting for them to order.

'I recommend the *merluza*,' said Gil, with infuriating calm.

The menu was simple, but everything was good. They were brought a bowl of tomato salad dressed in oil, for starters, and then the fish, huge, meaty steaks in a spicy sauce, with fried potatoes, home-baked bread, and wine.

'I suppose you eat here quite often,' Cordelia remarked, trying to steer the conversation back to an inoffensive subject.

'Lord, no. I can't afford to eat out all that often,' he replied matter-of-factly, without a trace of self-pity.

Cordelia allowed herself a triumphant smile.

'You could, as Lord de Mornington,' she pointed out. 'The estate has a number of financial holdings, in addition to the house and land. As I understand it, you would be quite wealthy.'

He set down his knife and fork emphatically.

'Miss Harris—Cordelia?' he said, pleasantly but quite firmly. 'We're two virtual strangers, passing an hour or so in each other's company, an event unlikely to be repeated—am I correct?'

'I should think that's a reasonable assessment,' she agreed carefully.

He nodded briskly. 'In that case, we can spend that short space of time in tolerable amicability, discussing any subject under the sun—the greenhouse effect, world politics, utter trivia—any subject other than the de Mornington estate. I've said my last word on that tonight. Understand?'

Cordelia sipped her wine, measuring the strength of his determination over the rim of her glass. He was still

smiling, but only just—his lips were compressed, his eyes
narrowed. He was not a man to provoke into anger, she
thought, sensing volcanic forces beneath the calm
surface. To probe too deeply and disturb them would
be to play with fire.

Why then did she have this strange reluctance to give
up on him? Was it simply her stubborn streak which
objected to conceding him the victory? Or something
else—a persistent if illogical feeling that she was arguing
not against him, but *for* him, in his own larger interest?

'Very well then—Gil,' she replied sweetly. 'I'll say no
more on the subject tonight. But tomorrow—to echo a
famous film—is another day.'

His laughter was harsh.

'I doubt it. Unless you're outside here tomorrow
morning, kitted up for a full day's walking in the mountains, you won't be talking to me at all,' he said triumphantly. 'By the time I get back, you'd be well advised
to be back in Castro Urdiales, where you may return this
to Mr Penfold. Having provided me with an excuse to
have dinner with you, it has served its purpose, I feel.'

He reached inside the pocket of his shirt and withdrew
the manila envelope, unopened, which he laid very precisely and deliberately on the table beside her plate.

'Oh, and do give my love to Merche,' he added, with
a reminiscent smile of such blatant sensuality that
Cordelia felt her skin tingle with sensations at the same
time discomfiting and pleasurable.

Go up into those lonely, fearsome mountains with this
man? That would be an act of sheer lunacy, since she
scarcely knew which of them disturbed her the most.

And anyhow, she did not have any shoes.

CHAPTER THREE

CORDELIA slept surprisingly well—it must have been the wine, she thought. But she was wide awake and ticking by seven-thirty, and she could only suppose her subconscious mind had been hard at work while she was asleep, for she knew exactly what she was going to do, without being aware of having made a decision.

She got up, washed, and put on her jeans and sweatshirt. There was a warm sweater of Bryce's in the car, so she commandeered that too—now her only hurdle was the shoes. She had only sandals with her.

She had noticed yesterday that there was a shop in the village which looked as if it sold everything, the kind of all-purpose general store fast vanishing from English villages, where everyone now had access to a supermarket. Before she even thought about having breakfast, Cordelia set off determinedly for the shop.

Casa Antonio was in fact half shop, half bar, a long counter running down one side, behind which a coffee machine hissed, and bottles of cider and brandy were ranged, along with a couple of beer pumps. Huge sides of cured ham hung suspended on hooks from the ceiling, and on the counter were great slabs of the local cheese which Gil had pressed Cordelia to try at dinner last night—creamy and blue-veined, like Stilton, but salty and far stronger.

At the far end of the shop were more shelves, stacked not only with tins of food, but with thick sweaters, socks, and yes—shoes! However, Cordelia knew success was far from assured. She took an English size four, not an easy fit back home. Here—who knew? Her hopes might well be dashed right now, and to save her life she could not have said if that would disappoint or greatly relieve her.

Antonio had innumerable pairs of strong walking shoes, essential in this kind of country. Not just one, but several fitted Cordelia, much to her surprise. Antonio, who had a few words of English, explained to her that many Spaniards had small feet, and here she was not unusual.

Kitted out in her walking gear, her apprehension increasing by the minute, Cordelia trotted back to the hotel, where she found a small party of people similarly attired, but as yet, no sign of Gil.

There was just time to phone Bryce and tell him her intentions.

'I'm going to have one more crack at our unwilling peer of the realm,' she announced. 'I'm going walkies in the Picos. Wish me luck!'

'You're to do no such thing, Cordelia!' he all but squealed. 'You can't go running off into the mountains—I'm sure it's not wise!'

In her heart she thought he was probably right, but his attempt to order her about only made her more determined.

'Oh, come on, Bryce, it can't kill me,' she said briskly.

But as she joined her fellow walkers, smiling politely at them, her own doubts multiplied. She was not the kind of person who did this sort of thing. True, she went out into the country to paint, but she took her car, never walked further than she could carry her easel, and Herefordshire had a far more gentle terrain than this.

From what she could discern, the rest of the group appeared competent and unworried, as if they walked regularly for the pleasure of it, which was probably the reason why they were here. There was a party of four young men who sounded as if they were Dutch, two well-set-up Spanish ladies in their thirties who looked like schoolteachers, and a middle-aged American couple, alarmingly fit and athletic. Could she, inexperienced and sedentary, keep up with these seasoned experts?

'Well, well!' A drawling voice behind her made her jump, and she turned to see Gil regarding her with faint mockery. 'Decided to join us, have you? Ten out of ten for determination, Cordelia!'

He introduced everyone in the group to everyone else, in Spanish and English—fortunately, the Dutch party could get along tolerably well in the latter—then signalled to Luis, who came running out with a tray bearing steaming coffee and hot chocolate, plates of fresh bread, butter and jam.

'No one walks with me on an empty stomach,' said Gil. He looked more rugged than ever this morning, in jeans and a chunky sweater, and looking Cordelia over quickly, he went to a Land Rover parked nearby and produced a small rucksack.

'This I can loan you,' he said. 'There are some socks inside—put them on. Yes, I know it feels too warm for them right now, but your feet will blister if you don't. There are also spares, a sun-hat, and a set of waterproofs. It can rain damn hard and unexpectedly up there, although the forecast is good.'

Smiling round at the assembled party as they all tucked in to breakfast, he said, 'Today's walk is really no more than a pleasant stroll—yes, I promise you!'—as several dubious laughs punctuated his words. 'We're going to head up over the shoulder of the hill over there—drop down into the valley of the Cares river, follow that for a while, then climb a short way to a village which can only be reached on foot.'

He spread out a map on the table, identified a peak, then pointed dead ahead into the sheer, blue-green distance.

'The mountain you see there, shaped like a section through a cut orange, is the Naranjo de Bulnes. You'll be seeing it at closer quarters later. Right? Everyone ready?'

Everyone was ready, even eager, except for Cordelia, who tagged along at the tail of the party as they followed Gil up a steep path leading out of the village. Very soon, La Vega was a toytown far below, and then it disappeared completely over the shoulder of the hill. They climbed upwards into a high blue solitude which seemed to be inhabited only by the song of birds and the humming of insect life in the grass. All around them, the peaks rose theatrically, wrapped in the mystery of their distant heights.

It was as if they were alone in the world, where no one had trod before, when suddenly, round a bend in the path, appeared a small party consisting of a young man with a dog, a small child, two black-clad, very elderly women—and a pig!

'You see!' laughed Gil, as everyone said, *'Olà!'* as they passed. 'Didn't I tell you it was just a stroll? The villagers have trekked regularly between these mountain settlements since long before there were roads.'

Cordelia wondered exactly where the little group had walked from. As they went on, here and there they passed small stone dwellings half hidden on the wooded slopes, mostly empty now, but once someone must have lived in them. What an isolated life they must have led! She shuddered briefly, and found Gil walking alongside her, observing the tremor of her shoulders.

'You really don't like the mountains?' he asked, as though this were a heresy hard to comprehend.

'I find them frightening and oppressive,' she replied honestly. 'Some famous writer—I can't remember who— once said that mountains are for looking up *at*, not down *from*, a sentiment with which I entirely agree.'

'Then why have you come today?' he demanded directly.

'I wanted to talk to you, and this seemed to be the only way.'

He sniffed.

'Very laudable. I admire your spirit, but I have to tell you that you're wasting your time.'

'But why, Gil?' she pressed. 'What does it cost you to read your father's will? To talk to Bryce? Nothing! You can't just turn your back on your heritage.'

'Can't I?' Dark eyes regarded her challengingly. 'It very successfully turned its back on me for more than twenty-five years.'

He paused, considering briefly whether he wanted, or even needed, to say more. Then he went on, 'It's not really any of your business, but since you've put yourself out this far, I'll tell you. My so-called father met my mother here when he was a student, on a climbing holiday. Since she was a well-brought-up, quiet Spanish girl from a good family, the only way he could have her was to marry her, which he did.'

His voice dropped, became deep with contempt.

'He took her youth, gave her a child, and then, when he'd finished with her, he discarded her.'

There was pain to be discerned in the hard depths of his eyes, and Cordelia did not doubt the strength of his feelings.

'Were they... were they divorced?' she asked quietly, almost afraid to question him for fear of an explosion. But he answered her levelly enough.

'No. She'd committed no offence, and divorce for no valid reason was not so easy then. Remember that she was a good Catholic girl. But he broke her heart. She was never strong, and she died when I was very young.'

Genuinely moved, Cordelia said, 'I'm sorry. That's such a sad story, and I can understand how you feel. But it isn't the present Lady de Mornington's fault, nor her children's.'

'*De acuerdo*—granted. I don't hold them responsible for anything, and they're welcome to the estate.'

'But the younger son, Ranulf, can't inherit. Only *you* can,' she pointed out. 'Gil, as I told you last night, apart from anything else, it would make you seriously rich.'

He laughed softly.

'Do I look as if that might concern me? Would I be living like this if it did? What do *you* do for a living, Cordelia?'

She hesitated, trying to fathom the point he was intent on making before she answered.

'I run a shop selling artists' materials, and a small gallery, which was left to me by my father, who also died recently. Whom I loved very much, and deeply miss.'

He raised and lowered his shoulders, not really a shrug, more an acknowledgement of their widely differing response to a similar situation.

'I'm sorry for your loss, but you were fortunate to have, well into adult life, the companionship and guidance of a parent with whom you were close,' he pointed out. 'As for this shop, I somehow have the feeling it doesn't satisfy your ambitions totally.'

How he had intuitively reached such a conclusion, from the little she had said, puzzled and disturbed her, but with his penetrating dark eyes fixed on her she found it difficult to dissemble.

'Not entirely,' she admitted, 'although I do enjoy the contact with people.'

'But your heart wants something else? What?'

She drew a deep and painful breath. This was hard to talk about; it hurt, and she resented it. But he had opened up to her, and somehow she could not refuse to tell him.

'I . . . I've always wanted to paint . . . but for various reasons I've neglected it lately . . . and it seems to have deserted me.'

His smile was compellingly brilliant.

'You mustn't allow it to,' he said, his eyes taking in the chiselled delicacy of her features, her slim, elegant build. 'I figured there was something unusual about you last night—with all that red hair loose, you looked like a work of art. And I've never seen eyes quite that blue before.'

Cordelia was thrown into a deep confusion by this descriptive and complimentary line of talk. No one had ever spoken to her quite that way before, and she would have been a strange woman if it had not caused her pulse to race excitedly. She had to remind herself that this was most likely a practised seducer, and she wasn't about to have her head turned so easily.

'What nonsense!' she said sternly, and Gil laughed, unperturbed.

'If you say so. But the point, from which we seem to have strayed, is that I live like this because I enjoy it, although it's unlikely to make me rich. I like being close to the land, these mountains, communicating something of my knowledge of them, my pleasure in them, to others.'

She would have liked to hear more about his way of life, but much to her disappointment he stopped in mid-flow just when he was at his most forthcoming about his reasons for not wanting the de Mornington inheritance.

'You must excuse me,' he said. 'I'm needed up front, I think.'

He left her abruptly, and she heard him identifying one of the myriad species of butterflies to the American, Hank.

It was very odd, she thought, but she could no longer say categorically, as she had said yesterday, that she did not like him. He annoyed and stimulated her. Certainly, he puzzled her, even now, when she had listened to his very reasonable explanations for his choices, and still felt there was a piece of the jigsaw missing, not accounted for.

But as they followed the valley of a rushing, chattering river, crossed it via a rustic bridge, and headed once more through verdant pastures and wooded slopes towards the higher reaches, her respect for him increased.

He undoubtedly knew these mountain tracks and passes unerringly, and he could stop and observe Alpine gentians and wild orchids, point upwards to where the vast wing-span of a griffon vulture hovered above the limestone crags, with ready ease, and a pleasant, totally unpatronising manner. Up here, in his element, he was easy to be with, easy to trust. Cordelia was sure they would encounter no situation with which he could not cope.

'There are bears and wolves in these mountains,' she heard him telling the party. 'But I shouldn't get too worried. 'You'll be unlikely to see them, as they'll certainly see us first. But if you look over there... at approximately ten o'clock, on that crag... see him? A chamois!'

They reached the isolated village in time for lunch, and by then Cordelia's feet and the muscles of her inner thighs were aching, for all she told herself she was a healthy twenty-two-year-old, and a bit of walking should not finish her off. She straightened up deliberately, determined not to let Gil see that she was tiring.

'All right?' he asked, coming alongside her, and she forced a smile.

'As you can see, I'm still here.'

'You'll be able to relax soon. We're going to stop here for lunch and a rest, before returning to La Vega by a different route,' he told her.

'How many miles will we have walked by then?' she asked tentatively.

'Oh, it's pointless to look at it that way. In terrain like this, it isn't the mileage, it's the up-and-down nature of it that counts,' he replied.

'Now you're being evasive,' she accused, and he grinned.

'That's right,' he said infuriatingly. 'The less you know, the less likely you are to collapse on the way back.'

She glared at his back as he went ahead of them into the village. Annoying man! She would make every step back under her own steam, if it killed her, if she had blisters up to her knees, she vowed. She would show him!

The village was no more than a scattering of houses set among cultivated fields, but Cordelia had to admit that its setting was pretty, and there was a peacefulness which came from the utter absence of wheeled vehicles. There were no made-up roads, only tracks, and everything, Gil told them, was brought in on the backs of mules, of which there were any number around, shaggy, appealing beasts which reminded her of childhood seaside rides, but here were a necessary mode of transport.

There was, however, a small *casa de comidas*, a very simple inn, where Gil had obviously made prior arrangements for them to eat, and equally obviously, there was to be no great hurry about it. Life here moved at a simpler, slower pace, and he had first of all to be greeted by virtually every inhabitant of the village, with much kissing and back-slapping.

They all sat out in the sun at a long trestle table, and while *lomos de cerdo*—hefty pork chips—were grilled over an open fire, a succession of cheerful women brought out hunks of bread, tomatoes and strong local cheese for everyone.

'Now for the *pièce de résistance*,' grinned Gil, as bottles appeared, large green bottles, and glasses more like tumblers, but with wide necks.

'Hey!' Hank said suspiciously, 'this ain't wine!'

'No, it's *sidra*—local cider, and it's fairly potent!' Gil stood up. 'The trick is to drink it like this——' He raised the bottle above his head, held the glass in his other hand, almost in the stylised stance of a flamenco dancer, and aimed a steady stream of liquid, unseen, over his head, neatly into the glass. 'A little at a time, then you drink it in one go,' he exhorted.

What an out-and-out exhibitionist! Cordelia thought disgustedly, forgetting that yesterday she had decided he was brusque and anti-social. She wished he would miss his aim and soak himself with the stuff, but of course he didn't. Clearly long practised in this art, he directed the cider perfectly, surely, into the glass, raised it, and downed the lot.

Of course, everyone wanted to have a try at this, with varying degrees of success, and much hilarity. More bottles were brought out, and happy pandemonium reigned. Cordelia watched, smiling, reluctant to attempt something she knew she would be unable to do properly, and unwilling to make a fool of herself in front of Gil.

'It's obligatory, you know,' he said, almost in her ear. 'You don't get your Brownie points unless you do the cider ceremony. It's Gil Montero's *rite de passage* for hill walkers.'

'Yes, no doubt, but I don't have many clothes with me, I'm sure to drench myself, and I can't drive back to Castro Urdiales reeking like an alcoholics' convention,' she protested.

'You won't, if you just do as Uncle Gil tells you,' he said, drawing her to her feet. Sliding one arm around her waist, he held her firmly, raising her right arm with his free hand. 'Tilt the glass at an angle...so...and pour into it.'

Cordelia could not move. All her awareness was concentrated on the feel of his strong, hard fingers pressing the small of her back, sending unaccustomed tingles of sensation up her spine. She tried to ignore the pressure of his hand, told herself that he was simply demonstrating how she could pour the cider, but it helped her not at all, for every nerve, every vertebra was sending mad, scrambled signals of pleasure to the next, all the way up to the nape of her neck, and down into her trembling legs. If she made a move, she was sure she would collapse in a heap, like a puppet when its strings were released.

Finally, it was he who moved her hand, directing the flow so that the liquid spurted neatly into it, not so much as a drop even splashing her.

'Now you're supposed to drink it,' he said, releasing his hold on her, seemingly amused by her statuesque immobility. 'Don't just stand there like the Venus de Milo!'

Cordelia, freed from the amazing, mesmerising power of his touch, gulped back the cider more quickly than she should have, and coughed. It was stronger than she had expected.

'I told you it was potent,' he laughed. 'Now, Madge——' he turned away, his humorous attentions diverted to Hank's wife '—you aren't expected to shower in it!'

Lunch was a cheerful, relaxed affair, everyone feeling self-satisfied by the achievement of having walked this far, inhibitions released by the cider, appetites sharpened by the clean, fresh air. Cordelia did her best to join in, but she could not prevent her gaze from straying to Gil every so often.

Was he conscious of the effect he'd had on her? she wondered ashamedly. Had it amused him to feel her tremble and then go rigid under his touch? If he could make her feel that way without even trying, it did not bear thinking about how she might react if he ever seriously tried to make love to her.

It had been a long time since she had felt herself even mildly attracted to a man. The last year or so, she had been so entirely preoccupied with her father's illness she had scarcely dated, her only and very occasional outings having been visits to concerts or exhibitions with close and caring friends. Before that, her painting had been her great passion, and she had never been strongly involved with anyone, to the point where she had been in danger of surrendering control.

To respond so fiercely to a man she had known a mere twenty-four hours, about whom her feelings were ambivalent, to say the least, had to be crazy. It had to be the sun, the air, the effects of this strange and frighteningly alien environment.

Tomorrow—back to civilisation as she knew it, she promised herself. She had tried to get through to Gil, on behalf of Bryce, and the unknown de Morningtons, and it would appear that she had failed. There was nothing more she could do, and she dared not stay here any longer, for to do so would be to put at risk something she valued and had always guarded fiercely—her own inviolate emotional detachment.

Cordelia was awoken before it was fully daylight by the loud, intemperate screech of a rooster somewhere in the village. Everyone hereabouts seemed to keep fowls, goats and pigs lived at ground-floor level in many of the old village houses, their body warmth helping, in winter, to heat their owners upstairs. Most families also had a few cows, which could often be seen treading the rough paths through the village to and from pasture, followed by a solitary man with a stick.

Now, after every rooster within a mile radius had added his voice to the chorus, the tinkling of the bells the cows wore around their necks prevented Cordelia from any possibility of going back to sleep.

Not that she could have done so, anyway, for her mind and her senses were full of yesterday—the dramatic gorges and pinnacles of the Picos, their immense green silence; the sunlit village, the cloudy potency of the cider. Gil's strong arm around her waist, the supple authority of his lean fingers... She stirred restlessly and rolled over to rest her head on one elbow.

She had returned dropping with fatigue, more than a little scared, but also elated. She had done it—she had walked a whole day where no roads ran, no vehicles could go. So her muscles ached, in spite of her precautions she had the beginnings of a blister on one heel, a patch of sunburned skin on her nose, and she would have given much for a long, hot soak in a tub, not merely a shower. But she had done it, and what was more, she wished she had had a sketchbook along.

So much so that after her shower she had sat down in her room at the *fonda* and sketched swiftly and compulsively, from memory, much of what she had seen that day, while it was still fresh and vivid in her mind. Flowers, crumbling old stone houses, towering peaks with a griffon vulture hovering over them...it was a long time since she had done any drawing which was not forced and desultory, and the mental sinews she now stretched hurt as much as the tendons of her thighs— and just as satisfactorily.

'I'm afraid you'll have to eat alone tonight,' Gil had told her, after their return from the hills. 'I'm invited out to dinner, and since it's at the home of the local policeman and his wife, I'd better turn up.'

'We're booked in at the *fonda* in La Vega for tonight,' Hank had said, overhearing him. 'It'd be a real pleasure if you'd join us for dinner, Cordelia.'

So she had, and listened to their stories of walking all over Europe, and how tomorrow they would be driving down to the Sierra de Gredos mountains, not far from Madrid. She tried to pay attention, but her mind kept wandering to her last few moments with Gil, before he had left her outside the *fonda*.

'You'll be heading back to the coast tomorrow,' he had said, not so much a question, more of a command.

She had forced a smooth smile.

'Trying to get rid of me?'

The smile which answered it had been deeper, more meaningful.

'Oh, no, Cordelia. I could enjoy having you around for a while, if you'd only drop this nonsense about the de Mornington estate,' he had replied, and she had felt again that strange stirring within her. What was the magnetism which drew her to this man, against her will?

'That's the only reason I'm here,' she had said forcefully, determined he should not run off with the idea that she had stayed on account of an attraction to him.

'Then you might just as well leave,' he had said brusquely, turning his back and striding off up the main street without another word.

The more she thought about it, the more Cordelia agreed that he was right. Both the man and this place disorientated and unsettled her. So why the faint, lingering reluctance? Wide awake now, she pulled on jeans and sweatshirt and, reaching instinctively for her sketchpad and pencils, crept quietly out into the early morning.

The sun was only just risen, but already the village was beginning to stir. She drew an old man with his three rangy cows—he merely smiled and said, *'Olà!'* unruffled by her activities. She drew the *fonda*, the huddle of small houses straddling the valley, with the Naranjo de Bulnes in the distance.

And then, without her having directed them, her feet found the pathway up to the house where Gil Montero lived—the Hänsel and Gretel house, as she called it. This time she captured it on paper undisturbed; only the tabby cat, curled up on a low stone wall, watched her without great interest.

The Land Rover was tucked away round the back of the house, so presumably Gil was in, but he need never know she had been here, she thought, as her fingers flew boldly over the page, seizing forever the essence of her fascination with this place.

Just as she had almost finished, the gate from the chicken pen was opened and Gil emerged with an empty feed basket in one hand. She saw his brow darken, and thought he was not pleased to see her. Whatever he had said yesterday, he would be glad when she had gone.

'What is this thing you have about my house?' he asked curiously. Before she could frame a sensible answer, he had opened the gate and was at her side, looking interrogatively down at her.

'I just wanted to——' she began falteringly, foolishly, but his gaze had dropped to the sketchpad, and his annoyance was suddenly transformed into an alert interest.

'That's not half bad,' he said, in grudging admiration. He bent over her shoulder, one deft finger turning the pages so that he could see the sketches she had done previously. 'In fact, they're pretty damn good. You did these flower drawings from memory, presumably, since you weren't sketching yesterday?'

Cordelia nodded, still speechless, dry-throated from the nearness of him. Wishing he would move away, and give her some peace. Wishing he would come closer still, even though she dared not imagine what she would do if he did so.

'They're surprisingly accurate,' he said. Then abruptly, 'Come inside for a minute. I want to show you something.'

Half of her cried out, no—leave now. He spelled only danger, and she could not cope with it. She had no experience of dealing with a man like this. But something—curiosity, or the magnetic pull she could not resist, made her ignore the cautious, warning voice of her own reason, and follow him obediently.

Pelayo thumped a friendly tail at her—since she had been admitted once by his master, she was obviously welcome, and not a threat. Cordelia wished she felt half as relaxed, but she couldn't, not with Gil standing next to her, and the four walls of his house surrounding them, cutting off her escape.

As before, his table was still covered in books, maps, papers and writing materials, but this time she took note, as he clearly intended she should.

'What is all this? You're studying something?' she asked, reckoning that to keep talking was her best protection.

'In a sense. I'm working on a guide book of the area.' He gave a brief smile. 'Not that there aren't any, but I think I'm in a uniquely placed situation to write one that's…well, if not better, at least different. And it gives me something to occupy myself during the winter months, when there are very few visitors.'

His very nonchalance somehow told Cordelia that this was not simply something to pass the time, but an en-

deavour very important to him. Hadn't she heard herself
using the same tone of voice when she casually admitted
to people, 'Well ... I do a little painting ...'

'You're a man of many parts, Gil Montero,' she said
lightly. 'I never had you figured as a writer.'

'I'm not one,' he said wryly, 'Only in the sense that
I know and love my subject. I learn the craft as I go
along. Nor am I a brilliant photographer, only ad-
equate, but I hope to have enough shots I can use to
illustrate. However——' he paused, looking down at her
with an intentness which made her breath catch in her
throat '—sketches such as you've done would be a marvellous contribution, especially for things like flowers
and birds, observed from life.'

'You mean line drawings?' In spite of her nervousness, she was interested in his ideas.

'Yes, maybe. And watercolours too. What do you
think?'

'I think it's a good idea, basically. You should be able
to find an illustrator to collaborate with you.'

He gave an impatient shrug.

'Are you dense, or something? I thought I'd found
one,' he told her.

Cordelia started, genuinely astonished. She had
thought he was only talking generally.

'You mean—me?'

'Of course I mean you! Why not?' he said, as if the
mere fact of his having thought about it meant she would
automatically fall in with his wishes. 'You're obviously
a more than competent artist, and you're already here!
Stay on a while longer. I'll take you up into the hills
again—sketchbook, easel, paints—the lot!'

Cordelia stared at him, speechless at first, not believing what she was hearing. Stay on here, among these
savage mountains, venture into them with him, day after

day? He must be crazy to think she would even consider it!

'I can't do that!' she said at last, when she found her voice.

'Why not?' His determined manner indicated that he was all set to override her objections. 'Do you *have* to rush back to Bryce Penfold? Is he such an impatient lover?'

She reddened with embarrassment.

'Of course not! How could you think such a thing? We're just friends,' she insisted indignantly.

'How could I think such a thing' Gil mimicked amusedly. 'People do become lovers, you know. It happens all the time.'

'Well, not to Bryce and me!' she exclaimed. 'The reason I can't stay is that I have a business to run. I can't leave it indefinitely.'

'You also have more important ambitions to pursue,' he reminded her. 'Do you mean to leave *them* on the shelf indefinitely? This place might just make an artist of you, if you gave it a chance.'

It seemed to her the greatest impertinence that he should delve about among her hidden doubts and insecurities, which were none of his business, never mind that he might be making a valid point. He had no right to make it.

'It's nothing to you if I ever paint again or if I don't!' she cried angrily. 'All you want is to make use of me, because I happen, conveniently, to be close to hand.'

And somehow, without her realising how he had done it, Gil had backed her up against the wall, blocking her exit with the solid firmness of his own body.

'Oh, I can think of much more pleasant advantages to having you close to hand,' he said softly, and bending his head, he touched her mouth very lightly with his.

She had not meant to respond, but her lips seemed to explode, to flower under his. He felt the shock waves that ran through her, and without hesitation, kissed her again, this time a long, thorough, searching kiss under which she gasped and drowned, going down, bereft of breath and no longer caring, as he carried her with him into uncharted depths of feeling.

His hands found their way under her sweatshirt at her waist, and worked slowly, exploringly upwards over her ribs, until his thumbs were tantalisingly stroking her breasts. Unconsciously, her body arched, tingling with sensation and silently begging for more. He gave it to her, but lightly, teasingly, as if she were a green novice he had to initiate slowly, his mouth savouring hers with exquisite, practised sureness, his fingers probing and caressing.

'I think we'd better take this thing off,' he murmured against her earlobe, and Cordelia came abruptly to her senses as he was about to pull the sweatshirt over her head.

'I think not!' she gasped, wriggling away from him, panting heavily.

He looked quizzically cool and unabashed.

'Why play games?' he asked calmly. 'You were enjoying that, and there are a million other... things... we could do, which I promise you you would enjoy equally.'

Cordelia, struggling with humiliation and a suffocating, unpleasant sensation she might have recognised as unsatisfied desire, had she been more experienced, stamped her size four foot furiously. She itched to slap his arrogant, attractive face, but a remnant of caution told her his response might be violent, so she contented herself with glaring at him.

'Oh, you're very sure of yourself, aren't you?' she exclaimed. 'Merche Ramirez warned me that you were no good—that you were the kind of man who only uses women, and she was right! Well, let me tell you this—there's no inducement you could offer which would make me stay here longer than another minute! As for working with you—I'd sooner be shut up with a rattlesnake!'

She stood, tense and white, still glaring at him, her breath coming in great, uneven gasps.

He put his head on one side, smiled at her with condescending amusement, then glanced pointedly at his watch.

'Your minute is up,' he observed drily.

She pushed past him and rushed out of the door in a fine, barely controlled rage, but as she stumbled down the path to the gate, he came to the door and called after her, 'Don't forget your sketchbook!'

She almost told him to keep it and use it to light the fire when it got cold, but something stopped her and arrested her in her flight, she stood at the gate, watching him as he came down the path, his stride lithe but unhurried.

To think that yesterday there had been moments when she had respected, trusted, and even tentatively understood him! Her first reaction had been a truer instinct—he was detestable, a man who preyed on women and treated them mercilessly.

'*Adiós*, Cordelia,' he said quite pleasantly, handing her the book.

'Goodbye, *Mr* Montero,' she replied acidly. 'I won't say it was a pleasure. In fact, I think Mornington Hall is infinitely better off without you!'

CHAPTER FOUR

BRYCE Penfold was not best pleased with Cordelia when she returned to Castro Urdiales.

'It was too bad of you, taking off when I was in no condition to object, ostensibly to deliver the copy of the will to Gillan de Mornington, and not coming back for three days!' he complained grumpily. 'What way is that to treat an old friend?'

She stared at him incredulously. After all the trouble she had taken on his behalf, to say nothing of the devastating treatment she had received at the hands of Gil Montero, this lack of gratitude was almost too much to take!

'It was to help *you* that I went in the first place,' she reminded him. 'Had you said you needed me here, I would have stayed. I didn't plan on being gone so long, you know—it just worked out that way. I thought there was a chance I could persuade him . . . it's not my fault that in the end I couldn't.'

'Hm.' Bryce was not mollified. 'I was beginning to think, Cordelia, that you'd gone and fallen for this man. I really couldn't see any other explanation for your absence.'

'Well, really!' she expostulated furiously. 'That takes the biscuit! I'm surprised at you, Bryce, for such unoriginal male chauvinist thinking! For your information, Gillan de Mornington—or Gil Montero, as he prefers to call himself, is the most arrogant, pigheaded, stubborn and downright devious individual I've ever had the misfortune to meet!'

61

'I'm not convinced you didn't have a sneaking fancy for him, none the less,' Bryce said suspiciously.

Cordelia bridled evasively. She couldn't, of course, put her hand on her heart and declare she had found Gil Montero wholly unattractive. All the same, her final judgement on him had been exactly as she had just stated. But she did not like the ring of possessiveness in Bryce's voice, so she said coldly, 'Even if I *had* taken a liking to him—if I'd decided to have a mad, passionate fling with him halfway up a mountainside, it wouldn't really be any business of yours. I'm a free agent, and can do as I please. I didn't, as it happens, do any such thing.'

'Hm,' he said again. 'That's as may be, but it was a mistake on my part to let you deliver legal documents. I wouldn't have considered it if I'd been well. You must have mishandled the whole thing. *No one* turns down a title and an estate like that. I shall just have to go and see the fellow myself.'

Cordelia could not resist a sour little smile.

'Be my guest,' she replied serenely. 'This time I'll pass. I'm not anxious to renew the acquaintance.'

Bryce took off in something of a huff, and Cordelia spent the next two days exploring the area by local bus, browsing around art galleries and museums in Santander, and avoiding the questioning glances of Merche Ramirez. That lady finally could restrain herself no longer, and burst out, one evening as she served Cordelia's dinner, 'You see Señor Gil? He is well?'

'I saw him. He's fine,' Cordelia replied non-committally. 'He sent you his...er...respects.'

Merche sniffed, her expression showing plainly her opinion of Gil's respect for anyone.

'He has lady?' she enquired.

'Not so far as I could see,' Cordelia answered carefully. 'He lives alone—if you don't count a huge dog, sundry cats and assorted chickens.'

It did occur to her, then, that in a village the size of La Vega it would be very difficult to live the life of a carefree Lothario without outraging local fathers, husbands and brothers, and, far from outraging anyone, Gil seemed to be on good terms with the entire community, including the local police chief.

But he had wasted no time at all in trying to seduce *her*. Perhaps he concentrated his efforts on female tourists? That, though, would surely do his reputation as a serious and trustworthy guide no good at all, and she had to admit she could not recall seeing him display any familiarity towards the other women in the party, on the day of the walk.

Only me, she thought ashamedly. Did he prey only on those who were alone and unprotected, who he thought were inexperienced and green? Her cheeks flamed. She certainly *was* inexperienced when it came to men like him! But she had to admit he must have believed she would be willing...she must have given him cause to believe so, albeit unintentionally. As she remembered that episode in his house, her swift response to his kisses, her too-evident delight in his caressing hands, her face grew hotter than ever.

At that moment she hated him for penetrating her previously firm defences, for showing her a wanton, sensual aspect of herself she hardly knew existed.

'You better leave this man alone, *señorita*,' Merche advised, drawing too accurate conclusions from Cordelia's pink face.

'You need have no fear of that, Señora Ramirez,' Cordelia replied fervently, but the fleeting hunger in the other woman's eyes told her something that surprised her—that Merche would have him back, none the less, if she could. Cordelia sighed, depressed by this evidence of the gullibility of her own sex, and vowed she would never let any man get to her that way, so that she wanted him, even while she despised the need in herself.

Bryce returned from his trip to La Vega unsuccessful.

'You met him, then?' Cordelia asked guardedly.

'Well, no,' he admitted. 'He wasn't there. He was away somewhere up in the hills. From what I managed to make out from people in the village, he was expected to be away for days—possibly even weeks.'

'He knew it was likely you'd come looking for him,' said Cordelia, unable to resist a mean feeling of triumph. 'Obviously he was avoiding you.'

'I can't imagine that to be true,' Bryce said, aggrieved. 'No one would behave in such a manner.'

Cordelia could not repress a chuckle.

'Gil Montero would,' she insisted. 'He made his feelings about the de Morningtons very clear.'

'Well, I can't hang around here for weeks,' said Bryce. 'The de Morningtons are important clients, but I do have others. There doesn't seem to be anything for it but to go home and report back to Lady de Mornington. She isn't going to be ecstatic—it leaves the estate still in limbo.'

And so they left on the car ferry to Plymouth, mission unaccomplished. All Cordelia had to show for the trip were bruised sensibilities and the sketches she had done in La Vega.

As for them, although they represented the first tentative stirrings of her long-dormant creative urge, she found herself reluctant even to take out her sketchbook and look at them, because they did not just remind her of La Vega, they reminded her of Gil. His hard eyes, his scornful voice, his frightening flashes of intuitive understanding. Most definitely, she did not want to be reminded of him, so she pushed the sketches into a drawer, and did not show them to anyone.

They had been back in England a matter of days when Bryce telephoned her.

'How would you like to come to tea at Mornington Hall?' he enquired.

'Me?' Cordelia was surprised. She had forgiven him for insinuating that she had somehow messed up the business of handing over the will, but there remained a lingering coolness in her. 'Why on earth should *I* be invited? They don't know me at all.'

'I know, but although I've explained the situation to Lady de Mornington, you're the only person here who's actually met her stepson, and she's curious,' he explained. 'She finds it hard to believe, as I do, that he simply refuses point-blank to communicate with her. It might help if you and she had a talk.'

Cordelia took a deep breath. It was going to be a very difficult matter to explain, with any tact, especially given the fact that Bryce still did not wholly believe in her side of the story, and from the sound of it, neither did Lady de Mornington. But she would not shirk it. After all, she had deliberately and of her own free will involved herself in the de Morningtons' problems.

'Very well, I'll do my best,' she promised, wishing, not for the first time, that she had never made that impulsive trip to La Vega.

It was a splendid September afternoon when Bryce picked her up outside her shop and drove them to Mornington Hall. They took the road north out of the city, following the valley of the Wye through countryside which ravished the eye, but gently. The leaves of the trees, ancient ash, oak and birch, were beginning to turn to gold and flame, setting the soft curves of the hillsides afire with colour, the distant outlines of the Black Mountains dark and mysterious by contrast. Cordelia inhaled deeply and contentedly—this was country she knew, loved and understood.

Bryce glanced sidelong at her.

'Are you ready for this?' he asked as he turned the car in between imposing, stone-pillared gates.

'This is the de Mornington estate? I've driven past it many times, but you can't see the house from the road,' she frowned. 'Where is it?'

'Patience,' he counselled. 'You won't see it for some time. This is only the deer park.'

'The—what!' she gasped.

It seemed to stretch forever, acres of wooded, hilly, verdant parkland. They passed a lake, smooth, grassy hills and graceful trees reflected in it.

'This part was landscaped by Capability Brown,' Bryce informed her.

'I never knew there was so much of it!' Cordelia mused, astonished.

'There's much more—any number of tenant farms, for a start,' he told her. 'The original land grant was recorded in the Domesday Book, and the family has been amassing land and possessions ever since—by marriage, by purchase, by gift from grateful monarchs, or as a reward for service in sundry wars. Look—you can see the house now.'

The house? Could one call it a house? Cordelia wondered. The core of it was an ancient, fortified manor, like a miniature castle, with towers at each corner, built from the local rose-grey sandstone. It was possible to see, in the lie of the surrounding well-tended lawns and terraces, where the protective moat had once encircled it. Generations since had added wings, from the mediaeval to the late eighteenth century, but somehow this medley of styles did not detract from the dignity of the building. It only emphasised the long continuity of its history.

She gasped. This was the heritage on which Gil Montero was intent on turning his back! A lump formed in her throat, and suddenly she felt unaccountably sad...sad, and angry with him, at the same time. She wished he could see it as she was seeing it now, for the first time, tranquil and venerable in the mellow September sunlight.

'It's beautiful!' she breathed.

She was still in a state of stunned bemusement as she got out of the car and walked with Bryce up to a front door, impressive on its own, but set in an aperture large enough once to have accommodated a draw-bridge...which, of course, it must have done, she reflected.

The door was opened for them by a sober-suited man in black, and Cordelia glanced quickly at Bryce. She had never before visited a household which employed a butler, and she wished he had warned her of the scale and splendour of Mornington Hall. She hoped, too, that her soft rust and green suit was smart enough for the occasion.

The hall into which they were shown was large enough to hold a dance in, but housed no more than a couple of antique oak chests upon which stood bowls of autumn flowers—chrysanthemums and dahlias in jewel colours. They crossed what seemed like acres of old gold parquet, and were ushered into a drawing-room.

Cordelia registered a quick impression of solid, comfortably upholstered furniture, long windows admitting views of the garden and streaming rays of sunshine. In front of the Adam fireplace—they had moved centuries, in seconds, from the mediaeval to the Georgian wing—two Afghans slept, opening lazy eyes to look at the new arrivals, then closing them again. She was reminded sharply of Gil's small house in La Vega, and of Pelayo—strange echoes from what seemed, on the surface, a different lifestyle...but perhaps, in some ways, it was not?

Then she turned all her attention to the woman who came forward to greet them, hand outstretched.

'Mr Penfold, it's nice to see you again,' she said in a low, cultured voice. 'And this must be Miss Harris. How *very* good of you to come, my dear. I'm Evelyn de Mornington.'

Lady de Mornington looked ridiculously youthful to have a son of Cordelia's age. She was slender and silver-blonde, although far from fragile—her hands looked well capable of controlling a horse, and she had the kind of bone-bred beauty which suggested she would probably still look good, and be active, into her eighties. A countrywoman, with a lineage as good as her husband's, Cordelia guessed.

'Could you organise tea for us now, Simpson?' she said pleasantly to the butler, and to Cordelia, 'Do come and meet the family.'

The little group around the fireplace looked for all the world as if they were ready to repel invaders—as if Bryce and Cordelia, far from being mere intermediaries, were harbingers of the invasion. She could feel the suppressed resentment emanating from them, and wanted to say, 'Look, don't shoot the messenger! It has nothing to do with me, and I'm not responsible.'

The Honourable Ranulf was a tall young man well over six feet, good-looking in a languid way, with corn-coloured hair flopping over his forehead. His sister, Gaynor, had the same fair colouring, and was tall for a girl. Cordelia would have described her face as pert, rather than pretty, but she would have appeared more attractive with a less petulant expression on her face.

'And this is Alyssa,' Lady de Mornington said, as the third member of the group detached herself slightly from her companions. 'She's a cousin in some complicatedly distant way I won't attempt to explain, and has lived with us since her parents died, some years ago. My husband was her guardian.'

The de Mornington features, which were handsome but unremarkable on Ranulf, and piquant on Gaynor, were translated into full beauty in Alyssa. Ironically, *she* could have been Evelyn's daughter. Her face was a fine, high-cheekboned oval, her eyes green, her hair long, flowing and silky. She was slim and lissom, her every movement catching the eye—and perhaps calculated to do so, Cordelia could not help but think.

'Do come and tell us all about your trip to Spain,' she urged in a breathy, husky voice. 'I'm just longing to hear more about the wild Spaniard!'

Ranulf gave a snort of hostile disapproval.

'The wild Spaniard, as you so carelessly term him, has cheated me out of Mornington Hall,' he reminded her. 'I do think it was too bad of my father to have kept all this from us for so many years.'

'Gosh, yes!' Gaynor piped up in agreement. 'It's all very well for you to be amused, Alyssa—you weren't going to inherit, anyhow.'

'Nor were you, darling, as a mere female!' Alyssa retorted, a gleam of malice in the green eyes. 'The worst our new overlord could do would be to cut your allowance so you couldn't spend so much on clothes, which would be no bad thing. You might learn some taste.'

The point was no less cruel for being well made. Gaynor's tight black leggings made her look thinner than necessary, and the shrieking orange of her long tunic washed out her quiet colouring. Alyssa, on the other hand, wore a soft silver-grey sweater tucked into fluid charcoal pants, which only emphasised her striking fairness.

'Alyssa! Children!' Lady de Mornington remonstrated mildly, but with some distress. 'That will do, please—I will not have bad manners in front of guests.'

She turned apologetically to Cordelia. 'I'm afraid you caught us in the middle of a—a discussion of our changed circumstances, which isn't an infrequent occurrence these days. This business is making us all rather edgy.'

A moment ago Cordelia had surprised herself feeling a sneaking kinship with Gil Montero. But, endeavouring to remain objective, she told herself that this was a family under severe strain. All their expectations and beliefs had been overturned instantly on the death of Giles de Mornington, and it could not be easy for them to adjust to the shock of learning that nothing was as it had always seemed.

They fell silent as a maid brought in the tea tray.

'All right, Julie, I'll pour,' Lady de Mornington said. The china was wafer-thin Crown Derby, and Cordelia held her cup very carefully.

Lady de Mornington looked at Bryce, a despairing appeal in her eyes.

'Have you had any form of communication with . . . with my husband's son?' she asked.

The last words were enunciated very carefully, and Cordelia could only sympathise, wondering what it must be like to learn that your husband had kept secret the small matter of an earlier marriage. She could well imagine that Evelyn de Mornington had been devastated by the discovery, but all the same she maintained an outward composure which had to be admired.

'I've heard nothing further, I'm afraid, although I have of course written,' he told her. 'As I told you, according to Cordelia, he seems most reluctant to involve himself in the matter at all.'

Four pairs of expectant eyes turned their attention to her, and she swallowed nervously.

'Yes, that's so,' she confirmed. 'In fact, it's an understatement. He left me in no doubt, he's adamant that he wants nothing to do with it.'

'In that case, can't we just rule him out?' Ranulf exclaimed impatiently. '*I* can be Lord de Mornington, as I always expected to be, and he can stay in Spain and climb mountains, or whatever it is that he does. Hey presto—everyone's happy!'

'Unfortunately it isn't quite that simple, legally,' Bryce began, and Ranulf thumped the low table, causing the Crown Derby cups to dance a jig.

'It never is simple, with you legal chappies!' he said distastefully.

'Ran, I'm sure Mr Penfold knows what he's talking about,' Evelyn said placatingly. 'We may not like it, but the law is the law.' She turned to Cordelia once more. 'Tell me, Miss Harris, what sort of man is he, this Gillan?'

Cordelia thought very carefully. Sitting here talking about Gil, when he was not present to put his side, made her feel oddly treacherous. But why should it? It was no one's fault but his own that he wasn't here. All the same, she weighed her words very carefully when she spoke.

'He's very... independent. Self-contained,' she said. 'I have to say that he feels some resentment. Not towards any of you,' she added hurriedly, 'but towards his father, who he claims abandoned him and his mother when he was a child. He considers himself a Spaniard, for all he speaks English fluently and was educated here. He lives alone in a remote village, from where he takes parties trekking in the mountains.'

'How very romantic,' Alyssa drawled wickedly. 'I think I'd rather like to meet him! He sounds fascinating! And you say he lives alone, so presumably he isn't married?'

Cordelia was visited by a sudden uncomfortable vision of Gil and Alyssa together, his brooding darkness, her blonde beauty, perfectly complementary. She was surprised by the painful twist of her guts this image caused.

'No, he's not married,' she said shortly. 'I would say he's probably not the marrying type.'

Alyssa's fair, well-shaped eyebrows rose.

'More and more interesting! I'm positively intrigued,' she breathed. 'Is he good-looking? Did *you* find him attractive?'

Cordelia floundered, and Evelyn came to her rescue.

'Alyssa!' she reproved her. 'Do stop interrogating poor Miss Harris. Besides, whether or not this man is handsome is hardly relevant. Have a fairy cake, Miss Harris—they're excellent. Cook made them freshly this morning.'

Cordelia was just thinking, gratefully, that this hurdle had been avoided, when Gaynor jumped in gleefully.

'My cousin can't resist anything in trousers, can you, darling?' she murmured sweetly.

Alyssa pulled a face, then laughed softly.

'It's the other way around, sweetie. *They* can't resist *me*. But you wouldn't know anything about that, would you?'

'Oh, for heaven's sake, stop bickering, you two!' Ranulf snapped disgustedly. 'Miss Harris, I apologise for my sister and my cousin. Their problem is that they've never had enough to do with their time!'

Gaynor folded her long legs under her.

'Ran is feeling his position since Daddy died,' she said. 'Before that *he* never did anything but hunt and play rugby. Now, all of a sudden, it's all *noblesse oblige*, you know?'

Lady de Mornington looked as if she was barely holding herself together, lips compressed, forehead tense. All at once, she stood up.

'Please excuse me for a minute,' she said in a superbly controlled voice, and swiftly left the room.

'Now you've gone and upset Mummy!' Ranulf accused.

Cordelia saw Gaynor's eyes fill with unshed tears. Undoubtedly, she was an over-privileged brat, but she did have feelings. Alyssa, on the other hand, merely looked bored. The situation verged on the awkward, and Ranulf leapt into the breach, engaging Cordelia in a discussion about her travels in Spain, in which she eagerly complied, anxious to return the atmosphere to normalcy—or whatever passed for it in this edgy and stressful household.

Lady de Mornington returned five minutes later.

'I had to tell Simpson to order more tea,' she smiled, which was nonsense, of course, since presumably she could have rung a bell and summoned the maid. But Cordelia had to admire her iron command of her emotions.

Gil, she thought, with sober conviction, could make mincemeat of this lot! They had lived all their lives cocooned in plenty, assured that nothing would ever change, and, now that it had, they were like a rudderless craft, adrift on a rough sea. Lady Evelyn was still reeling from her husband's long deception. Ranulf was clearly unready for the responsibilities he claimed should be his, Gaynor was gauche and uncertain beneath her brashness, while Alyssa...well, Cordelia caught the unmistakable scent of a crafty minx with a talent for stirring, and an eye to the main chance.

But Gil...he had obviously fended for himself from an early age, and Cordelia, reluctant as she was to admit it, could not imagine a situation with which he would be unable to deal. Somehow, she knew, he could find a way to master this craft, turn it around, and set it back on course, although his fellow travellers might not enjoy the process. Cordelia could not help thinking that perhaps Gil Montero was exactly what they needed.

Driving back through the spacious park with Bryce, she said, 'Well? What happens now? The whole thing seems to be deadlocked.'

He shook his head.

'I honestly don't know, Cordelia. This matter seems to be getting out of my league. I shall have to pass it over to Mr Faulkner, who's had more experience than I have, but even he will probably have to take advice. There are precedents for individuals renouncing titles, but ducking out of the entire inheritance…that's another thing altogether.'

Cordelia frowned. Another thought had just occurred to her, less obvious, and somehow more disturbing. As she gazed around her at the spreading Herefordshire acres, it seemed to her that perhaps this land also answered a need in Gil, of which he might not even be aware as yet. But he never would be, unless he saw it. He might feel the lack, without understanding it, all his life.

Quickly she said, 'But no further steps could be taken in Gil's absence, surely? It wouldn't be right.'

'I thought you didn't like him?' Bryce countered promptly.

'That's not the point,' she said.

Bryce dropped her outside the Cathedral and she walked slowly through the precincts, up the cobbled alley of Church Street, and into the quiet Close which led to the back entrance of her shop. The same empty silence met her which had saddened and unnerved her since her father died, but today she hardly noticed it, preoccupied with her own thoughts.

Her flat was upstairs, looking out over a small square, with the bulk of the Cathedral beyond. In the tiny kitchen she put the kettle on, then changed her mind and switched it off again. She'd had enough tea for one afternoon. Going through into her living-room, whose walls were an overspill from the art gallery downstairs, she poured herself a large sherry, and before she had time to change her mind, sat down at her bureau and took out a pad of writing paper.

Dear Gil

I know we didn't part on very good terms, but please ignore that—it has nothing to do with this letter.

Today I went to Mornington Hall and met your stepmother and her family. It will probably cut no ice with you if I tell you they're all under considerable stress, and only you can put them out of their misery.

So I shall tell you instead about Mornington Hall, and how, until you've seen it, you can have no way of evaluating its beauty or its worth.

Here, something seemed to take hold of her, and she forgot that she was writing to that strange man, Gil Montero, about whom her feelings were so ambivalent. She found herself describing in lyrical terms the loveliness of the deer park and the grounds, the green hills, the shining blue of the lake, the golden leaves of the trees. The ancient tranquillity of the house, and the way it spanned the different ages of its long life, acquiring only more beauty and dignity along the way. She wrote about a life she had never really known herself, only glimpsed; English country life, with long windows overlooking spacious gardens, dogs asleep in front of the hearth, tenant farms whose families had held their tenancies almost as long as the de Morningtons had owned the land.

Was it just a little bit over the top? Or was it no more than the truth as she had seen it? Cordelia did not know, but she knew she was not going to change a word of what she had written now.

'You can't walk away from something you've never known,' she finished. 'I challenge you to see it first. You owe that much to yourself—if you have the courage.'

It was rather an abrupt ending, but she did not think their short, abrasive relationship called for much in the way of pleasantries, so she merely signed off politely, formally, 'with best wishes, Cordelia Harris.'

I still don't know why I'm doing this, she thought exasperatedly, but she stuck a stamp on the letter, and walked to the postbox with it straight away, not permitting herself the luxury of second thoughts.

Only later, the thought filtered through into her conscious mind that if Gil *did* pick up her challenge, if he came here, it was almost inevitable that she would see him again. Hereford was such a close, compact city that, even without his seeking her out, they could easily run into one another.

But of course, that had not influenced her actions at all, she told herself hastily... certainly, when she wrote the letter, the possibility had not been on her mind. Only now did it occur to her. She did not *want* to see him again, did she? He was rude and arrogant, and thought too highly of himself, particularly where his effect on women was concerned. He might misconstrue her letter, though, in his infernal conceit, believing that she could not put him out of her mind, and had sought any excuse to engineer a further meeting.

Oh, well, that was just too bad. The letter was on its way to Spain now, and there was nothing she could do to call it back. It would be best, now, to forget the whole business, to let Gil and the de Morningtons sort out their differences as they saw fit. It was not her world—and not her problem.

September ran into October, and it was not that difficult to put all that out of her mind, as she was fully preoccupied with trying to make her shop a viable concern. The winter months were always less busy, and for her, the summer had not been a good one.

For some time she had been toying with the idea of running a small tea and coffee shop alongside the gallery, to attract more customers and bring in additional income. Of course, this required a certain amount of capital investment, which she could ill afford, but she decided it was sink or swim, and she must take the plunge. There were long, hard sessions at the bank, raising the loan, then the builders moved in to do the necessary alterations.

She was too busy to worry more than desultorily over Gil's reaction to her letter. She had not told Bryce that she had written it at all, believing that he too would get the wrong idea, but on the few occasions when she saw him he said nothing about any new developments. The de Mornington estate was still locked in legal stalemate, so it looked as if Gil had chosen to ignore the gauntlet she had flung at him.

This disappointed her in a manner she had not foreseen. For all he had aroused antagonism in her, she had not thought he lacked guts, but now it did seem that this man, who tackled alone some of Europe's wildest mountains, was afraid of the past, and of the unknown. She had severely misjudged him, and after all, she would not be seeing Gil Montero again.

October was well advanced when her telephone rang one morning while she was hanging some new pictures in her gallery, carefully treading around the plasterer who was busy in the coffee shop area, whistling tunelessly as he worked. She all but fell over his trestle as she hurried through to the shop.

'Miss Harris? This is Evelyn de Mornington.'

Cordelia had already recognised the soft, cultured voice, and her breath caught. Had Lady de Mornington heard from Gil? But then, if she had, why should she telephone *her*?

'I know it's frightfully short notice,' she went on, 'but could you be free for dinner here tonight?'

'Dinner?' Cordelia all but squealed, trying to veil her surprise. She had met the de Morningtons only once— why should they want her to dine with them?

'I do hope you can come.' Evelyn's normally collected tones had a strange, fraught quality. 'I've asked Bryce Penfold and he says he would be delighted to bring you with him. Nothing formal. Just—just the family, and yourselves.'

Cordelia gripped the receiver, a fierce suspicion growing within her that they had heard from Gil. Her stomach churned uneasily, and she swallowed hard, re-membering that Lady de Mornington was still at the other end of the wire, waiting for a reply.

'Well, yes, I'm free, as it happens,' she confessed, not adding that, for her, dinner was usually a quick session alone with the microwave while she did the day's ac-counts. Unable to resist posing the question, she asked breathlessly, 'Lady de Mornington, is it...have you heard from Spain?'

'I can't say any more,' Evelyn said quickly. 'I have to go now. Eight-thirty tonight? I look forward to seeing you.'

Cordelia bit her lip as the line went dead. It *had* to be that. Why else? And if Gil had written, what had he said? He had not given *her* the courtesy of a reply.

She re-dialled immediately and spoke to Bryce, but he was a disappointing source of information.

'My dear girl, I don't know any more than you do,' he told her, sounding a little annoyed at having to admit it. 'Faulkner and Penfold certainly have not heard from Gillan de Mornington, and if Her Ladyship has she's being decidedly secretive about it. I can only surmise she wants to talk in person, so put on your best bib and tucker and I'll pick you up around eight, say? The word is that the cook at Mornington Hall is superb, so at least we'll get a good dinner.'

Food was the last thing on Cordelia's mind at that moment.

'Let's hope for your sake that she doesn't serve seafood cocktail,' she said drily, before ringing off.

She was in a flutter for the rest of the day. Not only was she on tenterhooks to discover if, and what, they had heard from Gil, but she had never been invited to dinner at a stately home like Mornington Hall before. It was all very well for Bryce to advise best bib and tucker, but she had not a clue what to wear.

Nothing formal, Evelyn had said. But what was formal, what informal, at such a place? The suit her hostess had been wearing when Cordelia had tea with them had breathed couture in a refined, understated manner, and she didn't think either Gaynor or Alyssa were stuck for the odd few pounds when it came to buying clothes. She herself, on the other hand, had nothing that wasn't off the peg.

After much dithering, she decided that if one's outfit was inexpensive, it was best to err on the side of simplicity, so she wore a plain black silk shirt-dress which she had actually bought for her father's funeral, and had never worn since. She winced as she took it out of the wardrobe, but her father's photo, which stood on her dressing-table, seemed to be smiling wryly, and she could almost have sworn he approved of its happier use. She dressed it up with a floaty chiffon scarf in mingled shades of pink, and her best gold earrings and chain, put her hair up, then took it down again, fearing the effect would still be funereal, despite the scarf.

Bryce was on the dot of eight, dark-suited and tight-lipped, obviously uneasy with the aura of faint mystery about the invitation. Both of us are out of our depth here, Cordelia thought soberly, as they drove through the darkened countryside. What strange kind of aristocratic game was being played tonight?

The gardens were all but invisible on this moonless autumnal evening, but light blazed out across the terraces from the windows, and they moved indoors into a soft golden pool as the butler, Simpson, opened the door to them. A maid stood ready to take their coats, and as Cordelia divested herself of hers, Alyssa came gliding across the hall.

'How lovely to see you again,' she said with deep insincerity, smiling her false, lovely smile at Cordelia. 'What a charming jacket—is it silver fox?'

Cordelia knew when she was being put down, but somehow she kept her dignity intact, and returned the smile.

'Why, no,' she said, in a perfectly friendly voice, 'it's imitation. I think killing animals for vanity is quite disgusting. The only thing that really needs a fox-fur coat is a fox—don't you agree?'

Alyssa emitted a hollow, incredulous little laugh, but she could not immediately produce a retort. Finally, murmuring, 'What an odd, interesting idea!' she was about to slide past them into the drawing-room when the door opened.

'Ah, I thought I recognised the voice of a lady with strong opinions, and a stubborn mind of her own,' said the man who stood, perfectly framed, in the doorway.

Cordelia recognised his voice too, and the lean-planed face with the dark, ever-changing eyes. But she would have been hard put to it, otherwise, to see in this suave, immaculate individual the mountain man from La Vega. Gone were the scruffy jeans and checked shirt, and instead he wore a beautifully tailored lounge suit of a subtle grey, somewhere between dove and charcoal, and a soft raw silk ivory shirt. The loose but well-fitting jacket was unbuttoned, he did not sport a tie, and the whole effect was elegantly fashionable. The English country gentleman, twentieth-century style, heir to a long, unbroken tradition, quite at ease, quite at home in his own country mansion, set among his own broad acres.

'Welcome to Mornington Hall, Cordelia,' said Gil Montero, his voice calm, his smile like cream, and the wicked glimmer in the depth of his obsidian eyes for her alone.

CHAPTER FIVE

FOR what seemed like an age, Cordelia was speechless with shock. Then, delving deep within her own personal resources to find the ability to react normally, she managed to say politely, 'Gil—what a pleasant surprise! When did you arrive here?'

They were joined by a smiling Lady de Mornington.

'Yesterday—and quite unexpectedly,' she supplied. 'But we were all sworn to secrecy for just that purpose—to surprise you.'

Gil held out his hand to Bryce.

'Mr Penfold?' he said pleasantly. 'I'm sorry we never did manage to make contact in Spain. I understand you were ill, and then when you arrived in La Vega, unfortunately I was away on a long trek, and couldn't be reached.'

Bryce looked puzzled and mystified. The glance he shot at Cordelia was questioning and faintly accusatory, then he smiled, assumed his best professional manner, and said, 'Yes, it was all most unfortunate. However, I'm very pleased to make your acquaintance at last, Lord de Mornington.'

Gil gave a slight wince, which Cordelia could have sworn was feigned.

'Oh, please—I'm not used to being called anything but Gil,' he said easily. 'All this comes as rather a shock to the system. Shall we go through into the drawing-room?'

He didn't sound in the least overawed, in fact, he led the way as though he had lived all his life in this house, and took it entirely for granted.

Cordelia followed in a daze. Adrenalin was flowing uncomfortably through her veins, and she felt that she was in the most acute danger. Could this be the man who had virtually ordered her out of La Vega, who had told her in no uncertain terms that as far as he was concerned the de Morningtons and their estate could take the direct route to hell? Gil was up to something, and she wished she knew what it was. Whatever, she knew instinctively that she was not going to like it.

A fire was burning cheerfully in the large fireplace tonight, the velvet curtains were drawn across the long windows, and lamps and wall lights glowed softly. Lady de Mornington wore an elegant sheath of midnight blue, sapphire studs at her ears. Gaynor was in red—she seemed deliberately to choose brilliant colours that overpowered her, while Alyssa was stunning in a toffee-coloured drift of a chiffon skirt, topped by a short, ethnic, sequinned jacket that screamed Rifat Ozbek. The Honourable Ranulf looked tall and smart in a suit with a maroon velvet waistcoat.

But it was Gil who dominated, and to whom everyone's eyes turned in overt fascination, standing before the fireplace, gravely playing lord of the manor in a performance that would not have disgraced the Royal Shakespeare Company, Cordelia thought suspiciously.

'Thank you, Simpson,' he said, as the butler poured sherry and left the silver gallery tray with the decanter on the table for refills. The decanters had been in the fridge, Cordelia noted. Not twenty-four hours in the house, and already he had instigated the custom of serving the sherry Spanish-style, well chilled!

'He turned up quite out of the blue, without any warning!' Evelyn de Mornington could be heard telling

Bryce. 'We were all utterly astounded! A little unnerved too, since we'd been given to expect some kind of...well, misfit, with a chip on his shoulder, and a grudge to bear.'

Her eyes rested with faint reproach on Cordelia, who gulped. But what could she say, when she was not being directly accused of anything, although the implication was there?

'But I——' she began wretchedly.

'Don't worry about it, my dear,' Evelyn said kindly, laying a hand on her arm. 'I'm sure you meant well, to warn us, and we can all be mistaken. However...'

'Do have another sherry, Cordelia.' Gil appeared at her side, decanter in hand, giving her no chance to defend herself. She turned to him, trying frantically to snatch a minute when they were not observed.

'I simply don't understand all this!' she whispered furiously. 'You told me you'd never come here—that you wanted nothing to do with it! You were quite definite. And now...and now...'

'Come now, I may have been slightly taken aback by the news that I'd just inherited a title and a property from a father I never really knew. Who wouldn't be?' he said smoothly, in a normal, conversational tone which everyone within earshot could hear, as she was sure he fully intended. 'You didn't take me literally, did you? Oh dear!' He grimaced with apologetic amusement.

As he refilled her glass, he murmured *sotto voce*, for her ears alone, 'You got what you wanted, didn't you? I'm here. *Bueno*—so now I'm going to do things *my* way. Don't interfere any further.'

Looking up into his eyes, she saw the familiar hardness, the ruthless, don't-meddle-with-me signs she knew she ignored at her peril. She wanted to shout—this man is an impostor! What he's saying to you now is not what he said to me in Spain, two months ago. Don't trust him!

But who would believe her, even if she had the nerve to make such a public accusation? He was being so thoroughly charming and amenable, they were all convinced. Even Bryce was obviously convinced that, as he had suspected all along, Cordelia had had it wrong in the first place. He never had understood how anyone could not be thrilled by such a legacy. She would only be wasting her time, and making herself appear even more foolish and misguided than she already did!

The double doors at the far end of the room were opened to reveal a magnificent dining-room, a vast, inlaid rosewood table reflecting battalions of fine Sheffield cutlery, and serried ranks of Waterford crystal goblets. Two fine silver épergnes and a matching bowl full of autumn flowers and ferns made an impressive centrepiece.

'Dinner is served, sir, madam,' Simpson announced grandly, including the new lord proudly in his address.

Gil offered his arm to Lady Mornington with natural-seeming gallantry, and she looked up at him with the beginnings of trust, a lonely, bereaved woman, thankful for a man she could lean on.

Ranulf, escorting Cordelia, gazed suspiciously down at her from his height.

'You had us all going there,' he told her quietly, with a hint of reproof. 'Given that I'm not thrilled by the notion of anyone else's inheriting Mornington Hall— this I freely admit—but he's a regular guy, not some half-crazed foreign weirdo, as you made out!'

'I never——' Cordelia began indignantly, but Alyssa cut in from behind.

'Naughty, naughty Cordelia!' she giggled huskily. 'Did you plan on going back to Spain and keeping him all to yourself? I can't say I blame you—he's absolutely divine!'

Cordelia had no chance whatsoever to deny this charge, as by then they were all taking their seats around the table. But it was obvious to her what had happened. Gil, for reasons best known to himself, had turned up at his ancestral home playing up to perfection the English side of his chameleon-persona—the regular guy, linguistically and culturally adapted. They had not seen, as she had, the other side of him, the bitter, angry man she had met in La Vega. Nor did they yet know the Spaniard buried deep inside him, who co-existed uneasily under the same skin. They had accepted him at face value, relieved to find him handsome, approachable, strong— whatever each of them most hoped to find. And she was cast as the villainess of the piece. At best, she had got it all wrong. At worst, she had deliberately misled them.

Cordelia thought she would never forget the acute misery of that meal. The food, as Bryce had predicted, was excellent, she recognised dimly, but to her it all tasted like ashes, and she had to fight the temptation to anaesthetise her suffering by allowing her wine glass to be refilled too frequently.

The eyes of the de Mornington ancestors looked down knowingly at her from the walls, some of them fair, like Ranulf, others displaying a darker, more Celtic mien, not wholly unlike Gil himself. She could see the unmistakable evidence of his descent. A heavy burden of forebears came ready made with this inheritance—one who had fought Owen Glendower, then married one of his kinswomen, another who had gone once more unto the breach at Agincourt. A naval commander from one of Lord Nelson's ships at Trafalgar, a younger son who had died on the beaches of Gallipoli. The history of England written in the faces on these walls.

And here, seated below them, the latest in the line— Gillan de Mornington/Montero, assured and witty, the man who had made her tremble in his arms in the mountain house in Asturias, who still caused that *frisson* of half-scared excitement to jangle her nerves as she looked at him.

I hate you, Gil Montero, she thought, for the way you've humiliated me tonight. I hope you suffocate under the weight of all that history. You may be many things, but an English gentleman you most certainly are not—nor a Spanish gentleman either!

Catching her eyes on him, he raised his glass, smiling sardonically. And then, seeing that for a brief moment he had her attention, and hers alone, he actually winked, slowly and solemnly. As if this were an amusing masquerade, no more. As if he had not publicly branded her a fool and a liar!

'You must have misunderstood or misinterpreted what he said to you in La Vega,' Bryce insisted on the way home. 'I've said so all along.'

Cordelia shook her head stubbornly.

'Impossible. You're not going to make me agree to that. I know what I heard, and there was no doubt about it.'

'Then if that's so, why has he become so amenable now?' Bryce demanded. 'He seems to be saying he only needs time to adjust himself to the notion of being Lord de Mornington, and that everything can be sorted out. If he'd had a change of heart since talking to you, and had come round to that way of thinking, surely he'd simply admit it.'

Cordelia had realised by now that there was little to be gained by arguing the point. She did not herself understand why Gil was here, if her letter had anything to do with it, and if it did, why he had deliberately set out to make her appear foolish.

'I don't have the answer to any of those questions,' she admitted. 'All I can say is that he's a very complex individual.'

'He seemed perfectly straightforward to me,' Bryce shrugged. 'I think you have some kind of phobia, or should I say fixation about him.'

Cordelia did not deign to defend herself on this charge. Her best hope now was to keep well clear of the de Morningtons, their inheritance tangle, and Gil in particular, to have nothing more to do with any of it. Heaven knew, she had enough problems on her own plate without worrying over this one!

One small incident had convinced her that she was not going quietly insane, clinging to a belief no one else shared. Just before they left Mornington Hall, she was in the cloakroom tidying her hair when Gaynor slipped in.

Oh, no—someone else come to harangue me about misjudging their charming new relative, Cordelia thought ruefully. But Gaynor studied Cordelia's reflection silently in the mirror for a while before saying quietly, 'You don't buy it, do you? Neither do I.'

Even then, Cordelia, her fingers already severely burned, was careful not to commit herself.

'I beg your pardon?' she said politely.

'Gil. I don't think he's altogether what he seems.'

At this, Cordelia turned to face the other girl, relief plain on her face.

'You . . . you don't like him?' she queried tentatively.

'Oh, I like him well enough. Who wouldn't? He's been unfailingly pleasant since he arrived here, and he's devastatingly attractive.' Gaynor shrugged her thin shoulders. 'He's my half-brother, of course, but I've learned not to let things like looks cloud my judgement. With Alyssa around, men don't usually notice me.'

Cordelia was aware of a furtive sympathy for this gawky girl who didn't know how to make the best of herself, and was forever conscious of being outshone by her lovely cousin.

'One has to admit, Alyssa is very pretty, but that isn't everything,' she ventured.

'No? Well, it's easy for *you* to say. You're pretty too,' Gaynor sniffed.

Cordelia smiled. 'Not like Alyssa. I just do the most I can with what I have, and don't worry too much about it,' she said. 'We have to be more than the sum total of our appearance, surely?'

'When you look like Alyssa, it doesn't really matter what else you lack,' Gaynor insisted. 'It's easy to see that she's all set to get her claws into Gil. She eats men for lunch and spits them out, so perhaps someone should warn him.'

At this, Cordelia's laughter rang out heartily.

'It's kind of you to worry about him, but I shouldn't lose any sleep over it if I were you!' she said. 'You'd be better to warn *her*!'

Gaynor looked closely and carefully at her.

'Oh, gosh, you don't mean that you . . . that you and he . . . ?' she probed interestedly.

Cordelia shut out of her mind that brief, shaming episode in Gil's house in La Vega, and shook her head vigorously. It would not do for Gaynor to think she had any interest at all in Gil. She might tell Alyssa, who would certainly find it amusing to tell Gil himself. Besides, nothing very much had happened, she persuaded herself. It wasn't as if she and Gil had had an affair.

'No, I'm not involved with him,' she said firmly. 'I just think he's more than able to look after himself.'

'Certainly, it's my opinion that there's a lot more to him than meets the eye,' Gaynor observed, and Cordelia upgraded her judgement of the girl. Spoiled she might have been, but she wasn't stupid.

'Far, far more,' she agreed. 'And I've now said all I'm going to say on the subject, since your family already think I'm certifiable!'

Gaynor grinned.

'I know where your shop is. Perhaps I'll look in some time.'

'Do,' Cordelia invited her. 'As from next week, I'll be able to give you a cup of coffee and a sticky bun for your trouble.'

At least, she thought grimly, there's one member of the de Mornington clan who doesn't think I'm completely off my trolley!

Still, for all she had told herself very firmly that she was going to put the entire business behind her, she could not help wondering from time to time, during the days that followed, what was happening at Mornington Hall. Had Gil succeeded completely in winning over his new family, and overcoming any resistance they might still have towards the idea of his inheriting? And did he really intend assuming the title? Above all, over and over, she asked herself why, *why*, when he had been so decisively adamant, when she met him in La Vega, that he would have none of it? She could not make sense of it, nor of him.

The Monday after her dinner at Mornington Hall, Cordelia opened her new coffee shop. Really, it was no more than a corner of the gallery, screened off by trelliswork and climbing plants, with a tiny kitchen annexed to it. But she advertised its presence in the local press, and outside the shop, and a steady trickle of customers, small but gratifying, began to use it. Some were regulars, who always bought their materials from her, but others were new to her, and not a few stopped to browse around the gallery after they had finished their coffee, so she hoped each aspect of her business would in this way boost the other.

One afternoon early in November, Cordelia was in her shop, watching the rain bucket down from a darkening sky on the virtually deserted street. Dispirited, she turned away from this depressing scene. It was highly unlikely that she would have any more customers today, and she was sorely tempted to shut up shop and go upstairs to the warmth and comfort of her flat, only she knew how annoying it would be for anyone who did seek her out to find the place closed at an hour when it was usually open.

To while away the time, she went into the gallery, where she began changing the pictures displayed on the walls, and she was standing on a chair, hanging a landscape she particularly liked, when the bell on the shop door rang.

'With you in a minute!' she called out. Turning, about to step down, she stopped, arrested in the act. Gil was standing there in the archway leading to the gallery, and although she knew he was living only a few miles away, and that she could bump into him at any time, the shock of seeing him, of knowing that he had actually sought her out, left her frozen, unable to move.

'I should come down before you fall off that thing,' he suggested with a faint smile. Stepping forward, he raised both hands, planting them firmly at her waist. His fine cream trenchcoat was damp, as was the glistening dark head on which she looked down; he smelled of rain and Aramis and healthy male, a wholly disconcerting combination.

'I can manage by myself,' she insisted hastily, but too late. He lifted her easily, sliding her down the length of his body and setting her on her feet.

'My pleasure,' he said lazily.

'I'm sure, but anything in skirts is your pleasure, isn't it?' Cordelia retorted caustically, annoyed with herself for being so shaken by the contact, and venting her spleen on him. 'There's no reason why I should be flattered.'

'You do yourself a disservice,' he said, taking off his coat, shaking the drops from it, and tossing it over a chair. Looking around, he grinned rakishly. 'So this is where you keep the wheels of art turning.'

'They aren't turning with any noticeable enthusiasm this afternoon. I was about to close,' she said pointedly, snatching at an escape route. She did not fancy the idea of being closeted in here with him, with the rain teeming down outside. Or perhaps, subconsciously, it appealed to her too much, and her rational mind knew she should avoid it?

'Ah, but now you have A Customer, so you can't,' he said, with satisfaction.

'You can't mean you're actually going to buy something?' she said scathingly, and Gil laughed appreciatively.

'Who knows? I'm a man of means now,' he taunted. 'I'll have a cup of coffee, to start with, and then . . . we'll see . . .'

Cordelia fumed inwardly, but she could hardly refuse him, so she busied herself with the coffee machine, a gleaming monster with which she had barely got to grips.

'I'm sure the end result will be worth the wait,' he murmured, as the hot liquid finally began to gurgle into the cup.

Cordelia eyed him sourly as she set the cup down on one of the small tables. He was dressed in an impeccable suit of fine tweed, a soft shirt, handmade leather shoes; he looked and smelled expensive, everything about him making a statement of quality and taste.

She hardly knew what came over her—anger, pique, a fierce desire to avenge herself for the way he had made a fool of her at the de Morningtons' dinner, but before she could get a hold on her tongue, she heard herself saying with a mean triumph, 'You're looking very different these days, Gil. Very upmarket. I see you couldn't wait to get your hands on the de Mornington money you so much despised.'

The instant the words left her lips, she knew they had been inadvisable. His brow darkened until it was almost as thunderous as the sky outside the windows, and she saw, again, the bitter, passionate Spaniard, who looked as if at any moment he would close both hands around her throat and wring the life out of her.

Then he gave a wry, cynical shrug, and was once more the nonchalant English aristocrat.

'That's a typical statement from you: rash, ill-considered, and with no basis in fact,' he said contemptuously. 'But if you must know, the new wardrobe was financed from the publishers' advance on my guide book. I thought it would be ill-mannered to turn up at Mornington Hall dressed as Worzel Gummidge.'

'How considerate of you,' Cordelia said thinly, in no frame of mind to apologise for her error. He had dealt too deviously with her to merit clemency. 'I'm sure your new family were quite bowled over by your veneer of urbane sophistication.'

'They were highly relieved to find I wasn't a cross between Genghis Khan and the Abominable Snowman,' he said, with dour amusement. 'I must say you prepared the ground very well, Cordelia.'

She glared at him with unconcealed indignation.

'I thought what I told them was admirably restrained,' she retorted. 'I could have said what a misanthrope you were. I could have said that you were a shameless womaniser, without mercy or morals.'

He laughed mirthlessly.

'Not in front of witnesses, you couldn't. That's slander, unless you can prove it,' he said. 'Which you can't. I had an affair with Merche Ramirez, in which she collaborated more than willingly—this I admit. I also made a pass at you, which you all but invited, and most certainly didn't dislike. Only prudery and cowardice prevented you from falling into my bed.'

A gasp of outrage escaped her.

'That's out of order, and you know it!' she cried. 'I wouldn't fall into bed with you if the alternative were lifelong celibacy!'

'Sure of that, aren't you?' Gil enquired lightly. The dark arch of his brows, the odd look in his eyes, the gloomy seclusion of the gallery where only the spots illuminating the paintings glowed, all combined to evoke an atmosphere of danger and sensuality. Once again she was leaning weakly against a wall, cornered, once again he was looming over her, and she felt her will to escape, to resist, fading. She knew she wanted him to kiss her, but she didn't want to consent to it, for that would prove him right. She wanted to be overpowered, so that she could then say, I didn't want to...but he forced me.

He looked down searchingly into her eyes, and her heart sank shamefully as she realised he had read her all too well.

'Oh, no,' he said softly, 'I'm not going to give you grounds for shouting "rape!". I shan't touch you without your express permission, and I certainly wouldn't make love to you unless you invited me to.'

'In writing?' she asked cuttingly, and he gave a low laugh, easing away from her so that she could breathe again without that odd constriction in her throat.

'Perhaps not,' he conceded. 'A verbal request will do.'

'You'll have a long wait. It's not going to happen, either way,' Cordelia said clearly. 'I'm not lusting after you, Gil. It's just your infernal conceit that makes you think you're irresistible to women. All I want from you is to know why you're here, after all that you said in La Vega.'

Again, the casual shrug.

'I'm here to see my publisher. That seems reason enough to me.'

She gave a little cry of exasperation.

'You know what I mean! Why did you come to Mornington Hall? I simply don't understand.'

'Don't you?' His expression had hardened again, so had his voice, and she shivered at the menace in it. 'Well, you should. Didn't you write me that letter guaranteed to stir a response in anyone who wasn't already dead?' He jabbed an accusing finger at her. 'You really know how to turn the knife in the guts, don't you—describing so evocatively what I'd been deprived of since childhood? Oh, yes, and that was a nice final touch, wasn't it—appealing to my courage, or lack of the same? I expect you know that's a taunt no Spaniard can resist!'

Cordelia's eyes were wide with genuine amazement. She had written that letter to him unthinkingly, dazzled by her first visit to Mornington Hall, inspired by a vision of what it could mean to him. She had not intended it to be hurtful. He had put on so hard, so invincible a front that she had forgotten the occasional fleeting pain in his eyes, the long bitterness of rejection he must still resent. She had overlooked the simple truth that he too was human, and could suffer. And yes, she had issued him a challenge, but without understanding that he would take it almost as a point of honour!

'I'm here, *señorita*, primarily because of *you*,' he said, his voice low and cold with anger. 'And let me tell you, so that you never make the mistake again, that I do not care for being manipulated. *Claro?*'

And now she knew why he had behaved as he had towards her at the dinner party, why he had shown her up and made it appear to everyone that she had got the wrong end of the stick, or for reasons of her own had deliberately lied about him.

Revenge, they say, is a dish best eaten cold, Cordelia thought grimly. And Gil had certainly plotted and carried out his vengeance with icy forethought and precision.

'And...and now?' she asked falteringly, too shaken to fight back. 'What will you do? Will you stay, take your place as Lord de Mornington...or go back to Spain?'

He shook his head, and briefly, she surprised a lost, uncertain look in his eyes.

'I don't know,' he said shortly. 'Damn you, I don't know! You got me here, but now I have to find my own answers, and they don't depend on you! So keep out— and don't meddle in matters beyond your understanding.'

He took a deep breath, and once more his face was casually humorous. He reached above her head and took down a miniature from the wall.

'Wrap this for me,' he ordered. 'It just might amuse Alyssa.'

After he had disappeared into the rain once more, the handsome coat slung casually over his broad shoulders, Cordelia locked and bolted the shop, regardless of time, fled upstairs to her flat, and locked that door too.

She could not have said why she was virtually barricading herself in, at this time of day. Gil had been and gone, like a thunderstorm, he was unlikely to come back, and the damage to her nerves, to her self-confidence, was already done. All she was doing was trying to give herself a false sense of security, because she knew very well that the danger which threatened her could not be banished and locked out. It was already here, within herself.

I hate him! she thought ferociously, shivering despite the crackling flames of the fire she had just lit. But she knew that the truth was far more complex than that. Simple hatred would have been a splendidly straightforward emotion, with which she could have coped quite well.

What she felt for Gil Montero could not be dismissed so easily. Certainly she feared him—because he had assumed, as of right, a power over her that she had not willingly given him. He stirred her senses as no man had ever done, draining her of her will to resist him, so that each time they met she was obliged to fight a battle with herself.

And he doesn't even want me that much, she thought disgustedly; he just thinks he can have any woman, simply for the asking. She would be no more than another notch on his bedpost, quickly forgotten. Hadn't he already hinted at an interest in his cousin Alyssa? A perfectly matched pair, she decided grimly. Perhaps they would annihilate each other?

She made herself coffee, and sat on the rug in front of the fire, gazing worriedly into the flames, wondering why it was that she could not stop thinking about him. Reliving the moment when he had lifted her down from the chair, his hard, mountain-toughened body against hers, filling her with an abrasive desire...and later, when she had thought he was about to kiss her, wanting it to happen. You should be ashamed, she told herself, after the way he treated you at Mornington Hall.

Finally, though, the image that remained in her mind, and would not be shaken off, was that strange, momentarily confused expression on his normally confident face... 'I have to find my own answers...' It was the brief, unwilling admission of vulnerability which haunted her, revealing to her a man torn between two worlds, and struggling to come to terms with a side of himself he had long denied.

Rightly or wrongly, Gil blamed her for bringing him face to face with this conflict, and he seemed determined to punish her. Did he believe he could do it by making her want him, callously taking her, then casting her aside? So far, he had only toyed with her, and already she had felt the power of his attraction. Could she stand firm against a really determined onslaught?

Her only hope, she thought desperately, was in keeping out of his way. She could not afford to concern herself with his dilemma. Her own was far too serious.

CHAPTER SIX

THE streets of Hereford were brightly decked out for Christmas, with coloured lights festooned from trees and shop-fronts, and a large Christmas tree taking pride of place in the city centre pedestrian precinct. A light sprinkling of snow had fallen the night before, and some of it still lay on the rooftops, giving the place a seasonal air, and in the distance, the Black Mountains were freshly dusted with white.

Cordelia had done her Christmas shopping, but a good many people hadn't, and the shops were busy. Like many traders, she was run off her feet, and she did not complain as she flitted from shop to gallery to coffee bar, wrapping paintings, dishing out tea and cakes, and reminded herself it was all to the good—she needed the business.

'Gosh, you look frantically busy!'

It was Gaynor, warmly wrapped up in a quilted ski-jacket and leggings, the multi-coloured Aztec print drawing vivid attention to itself, and, as usual, quite overpowering her.

Cordelia smiled, abstracted, but trying to be friendly in spite of it.

'Yes, it's been rather hectic all morning. Can I do anything for you?'

'Well, no, not really. I just dropped by for a chat, but it looks as though you've got your hands full.'

'If you give me a minute——' Cordelia turned to attend to a couple dithering between which of two landscapes to buy. Gaynor had 'dropped by' a couple of times in the last month or so, and Cordelia had sensed a variety of needs in her. One, to get away from Alyssa; two, to talk to someone outside her immediate circle; and last but not least, to relieve her boredom. Cordelia felt a certain sympathy for Gil's half-sister, even though her own life seldom gave her time for the luxury of ennui, and she certainly did not envy anyone who had the constant yardstick of Alyssa against which to compare herself.

She had, of course, been more than curious to know how things were going at Mornington Hall, and fortunately, she had not needed to probe too hard. Gaynor needed little encouragement to expound.

'Gil? Well, I have to admit he's been a tower of strength,' she had said. 'I wasn't sure what he was up to at first, but now I don't know what we'd do without him. Mummy was in such a state after Daddy died, and Ran didn't know how to help her, but she absolutely relies on Gil, and he's marvellous with her. Almost like another son—only, of course, Mummy's not old enough to be Gil's mother.'

'How does your brother feel about that?' asked Cordelia. 'Doesn't he resent Gil for usurping his place in more ways than one?'

Gaynor shook her head.

'Funnily enough, they get on well. You know how Ran adores horses and hunting? He and Gil went down to the stables the first week and took out two of the hunters. Gil must have passed the test, as they've been thick as thieves ever since. I have to say, he rides like the devil,' she added admiringly.

Cordelia's eyebrows rose. Gil Montero does a lot of things like the devil, she could have said, but restrained herself. Trust him to possess the necessary skills required to fit in with his new family!

'He's spent a lot of time with Mummy and the accountants going through all the financial matters,' Gaynor confided. 'Mummy reckons he has a sound grasp of business, just as Daddy had. It's just as well, really. I mean, Ran likes messing around the estate, fiddling with this and that, but he hasn't a clue how the commercial side works. Gil soon got to grips with that. I thought you said he was dirt-poor, in Spain.'

Cordelia paused.

'No, I didn't say that exactly. I said he wasn't particularly interested in money,' she corrected. Obviously the talent had been there, lurking unseen in the genes. Perhaps Gil had not even suspected its presence himself, she thought uncomfortably, wondering what other hidden aspects of his own character he was unearthing in his new role.

'Do you know—the other day, he actually asked me what I was going to *do*—with my future, I mean,' Gaynor went on, her expression as puzzled as if the concept were entirely revolutionary. 'He said I was obviously bright, and had I thought of going to college! Then he went out and came back with a stack of brochures and prospectuses!'

'It's not a bad idea,' Cordelia agreed. 'All else apart, you'd enjoy it, and make lots of new friends.' Who wouldn't all compare you with your cousin, she added silently. 'What does Gil have in mind for Alyssa, then?'

Gaynor actually chuckled.

'He says she's a little more difficult, but he'll think of something!' she grinned. 'I reckon *she* already *has* thought of something, where he's concerned!'

Cordelia had tried not to wince.

'Do you think they're...attracted to one another?' she queried cautiously.

Gaynor shrugged.

'She flirts outrageously with him, and he teases her quite a bit, but it's hard to say what will come of it. He squires her around a lot, of course. Perhaps *he's* playing hard to get?'

And Gil, Cordelia reckoned, would want to call the tune, in any relationship. Alyssa was so beautiful, it was difficult to see how he could hold out against her indefinitely, given his track record, but perhaps even he would draw the line at making love to his young cousin under the family roof, even if she were eager to?

This conversation had taken place some weeks earlier, and Cordelia was not entirely sure if she wanted an update on it. Did she really want to know if Gil Montero's legendary charm had wreaked havoc on another woman—or if, this time, he had met his match? Certainly *she* had seen nothing of him. He had not been near the shop, apart from that one, unnerving visit. Perhaps he was so taken with Alyssa that he had lost interest in paying Cordelia back for luring him to England. The notion should have given her cause for relief, but actually, she did not care for it.

Sighing, she turned from gift-wrapping the landscape to see a good half dozen customers making tracks into the coffee shop, just as one of her regulars, who always had a large order for materials, came through the door.

She put on a bright smile, suppressing the desire to groan, and wishing, not for the first time, that there were two of her.

'Look here,' said Gaynor, seeing her dilemma, 'why don't I serve the coffees and so on, while you see to your customer? I don't know a thing about art materials, but I can pour coffee and put cakes on plates.'

'Would you mind?' Cordelia asked doubtfully.

'Lord, no, it'll be quite fun.' Gaynor stripped off her anorak to reveal an equally lurid electric blue sweater.

'Well . . . all right. There's a list of prices by the coffee machine.'

And then it seemed half of Hereford was either in the shop, just leaving, or just arriving. Cordelia sold, wrapped and cashed steadily, with scarcely a minute to see how Gaynor was getting on down her end, and an hour passed before they found themselves with a slight lull.

'Phew!' Gaynor mopped her brow. 'It isn't always this busy, is it?'

'Unfortunately not,' Cordelia grinned. 'It's just the Christmas rush, and I mustn't moan, I need all the business I can get! Is there any coffee left in that pot?'

They drank gratefully, and Cordelia was mildly surprised to find that the younger girl had coped quite well with her unaccustomed activity.

'I had a bit of trouble getting used to the till, and your coffee thingy is a mite temperamental, but I think I sorted it all out,' she said, sounding rather surprised herself. 'Gosh, aren't you lucky, having something like this to do every day? Sometimes I get so bored, deciding whether to go for a ride, or stay in and squabble with Alyssa.'

'Perhaps you should consider taking that college course,' Cordelia suggested.

'Oh, I don't know—am I really clever enough?' Gaynor frowned indecisively. 'I'll think about it after Christmas.' She brightened a little, picked up her anorak, and fished in the pocket. 'I really came to give you this— it's just a little present.'

Cordelia was touched as she took the slim box wrapped in glittery paper.

'That's very sweet of you,' she said, 'but I didn't expect——'

'It's nothing much,' Gaynor said deprecatingly. 'And look—if you're going to be this busy all week, I don't mind coming in and manning the coffee machine.'

Cordelia smiled gently.

'Gaynor, you were a real help today, but if you did that on a regular basis I'd have to pay you, and frankly, I can't afford an assistant.'

'Don't be silly. I don't need the money, and it would be fun. Look on it as doing me a good turn. I *need* to get out from under now and again,' said Gaynor, and Cordelia did not miss the faint note of desperation in her voice.

'Well, maybe just for an hour or so a day,' she agreed. 'If your mother doesn't object, that is.'

'Mummy won't mind. Why should she? She's still trying to work out how she managed to produce something like me, when she's so pretty and elegant! No doubt she'll have the house full of eligible young men over Christmas, hoping one of them will fall for me, but they'll all end up flapping around Alyssa,' Gaynor said practically, but with a hint of wistfulness.

And Gil? Cordelia could not imagine him 'flapping around' anyone. It was more likely he would just wait, dark and sardonic, until Alyssa got tired of all the boys and came to him as a supplicant.

That lunchtime, although she could ill afford it, Cordelia shut the shop and went to look for a present for Gaynor. Anxious curiosity had led her to open hers, and she was greatly relieved to find that it was a silver bracelet, set with tiny seed pearls—charming, but the girl had had the good sense not to buy anything too expensive, knowing she could not reciprocate.

She spent her entire lunch-break hunting, and finally settled for a soft, fluffy sweater in a delicate shade of powder-blue. Fully occupied for the rest of the afternoon, she was in the process of wrapping it prior to shutting shop, when the doorbell jangled and Gil walked in.

The shock to Cordelia's system each time she saw him never seemed to lessen. The room was full of him, her mind and soul were full of him; he dominated her existence to the exclusion of all other thought and sensation. What was it, this feeling that he induced in her? She could not identify it or give it a name, she only knew it was there, all-powerful, inescapable.

'Last-minute present-buying?' He looked down at the sweater.

'It's for your sister,' she said shortly, folding the gift wrap and tying the parcel with silver ribbon, concentrating on her task and trying not to look at him. 'She bought *me* a present—it was nice of her, but quite unexpected.'

'She admires you,' he said. 'Your independence attracts her. Fair enough, so long as she doesn't think she can run out and emulate it without any experience. I hope you liked her gift—she was a little unsure whether you would.'

'It's lovely——' She glanced up at him with a frown. 'But how did you know?'

Gil shrugged.

'She asked my advice. I had to steer her away from Cartier.'

'Well, thank *you*,' she said sarcastically, not at all thrilled by the idea of Gil explaining to Gaynor why it would be unwise to buy her anything too costly.

'*De nada.* I didn't want you to be embarrassed.' His smile was smooth, and betrayed nothing of what he was really thinking.

'This is new. I thought that was exactly what you wanted,' she retorted acidly.

He laughed.

'Oh, you're referring to my surprise party at the Hall? You aren't still holding that against me, are you?' he demanded softly. 'Come on, Cordelia—where's your sense of humour?'

'It wasn't funny, Gil,' she pointed out indignantly.

'That depends on one's point of view.' Head to one side, he regarded her, a wicked twinkle in the dark eyes. 'Truce? It's the season of peace and goodwill, after all. Shut up shop and come for a drink with me. We could bury the hatchet—preferably not in each other's backs.'

She had to smile, although she was not at all sure she believed in this conciliatory approach. He probably had some other devilment in that devious mind of his.

'I'm very tired,' she demurred.

'Exactly. It will relax you.' He took her coat from the peg behind the door. 'Come along.'

And somehow she found herself slipping her arms into it, saying grudgingly, 'Do you always get what you want?'

'Usually,' he replied cheerfully. His hands rested lightly but commandingly on her shoulders. 'It's far easier, and saves trouble, to go along with me in the first place.'

A shudder ran through her as his fingers deepened their pressure. He turned her round carefully, as though she were a puppet, and looked down into her eyes. The expression in his was frankly and intensely sexual. She was lifted on a wave of excitement by the awareness of desire in him, and had to remind herself firmly that with Gil this was meaningless. For him, the conquest was all, the relationship unimportant, and she had no wish to be another Merche Ramirez.

'Shall we go, then?' she said faintly.

'Whenever you're ready,' he agreed, and if there was a *double-entendre* in that she deliberately ignored it.

In the bar of the best hotel in the city, Gil ordered not just a drink but a bottle of excellent champagne, and smoked salmon sandwiches. In the warm, softly lit, lushly carpeted lounge, settled in a deep armchair, it would have been difficult not to enjoy this five-star treatment. It was difficult, too, to resist the spell of the man seated across the table from her, the virile invader, thinly veiled by an urbane and civilised veneer.

'So how will you be spending Christmas, Cordelia?' he asked, pouring more champagne and relaxing back in his chair.

'Resting,' she shrugged. 'Doing as little as possible, in fact.'

'Alone?' he asked, and she looked up sharply.

'Why do you ask? And what can it possibly matter to you?'

He sighed.

'Cordelia, don't pretend. I've been in your position for many years and I know how it is. No doubt you have many friends, as I did in La Vega, but Christmas is for families. You don't like to intrude, so you let each of them believe you're spending it with someone else. The reality is a good book and a chicken drumstick. *One* can't pull a cracker, and opening a bottle of wine for oneself is a swift route to perdition. Am I right?'

She allowed him to hold her gaze, her own eyes admitting the truth of what he said. It was her first Christmas without her father, and she knew she would feel keenly the loss of their quiet companionship at this special time. It was ironic that Gil, of all people, should be so acutely and accurately aware of how she felt.

'You're right, I suppose,' she said. 'But it doesn't matter. It'll soon be over.'

He leaned forward, shifted the bottle of champagne, and said easily, 'It doesn't have to be that way. Why don't you come and spend Christmas at Mornington Hall?'

Her surprise was so great, she could not stifle a loud gasp.

'Who... who's inviting me?' she exclaimed pointedly.

'I am, of course. That's my prerogative,' he said patiently. 'We have plenty of room, and Cook is catering for a small army. You're very welcome to join us.'

He spoke quietly, graciously, as if he had been issuing such invitations all his life, not simply for a matter of weeks. Already very much the master, Cordelia noted. Where, now, was that fiercely reluctant Gil she had crossed swords with last summer?

But to spend Christmas at Mornington Hall, and watch him playing this new part so superbly, dispensing drinks and hospitality? Flirting with Alyssa? Not a chance!

'It's very kind of you, but really, I couldn't,' she declined, politely but firmly. 'As you said, Christmas is for families, and this year you'll have yours. I should feel out of place.'

His laughter was suddenly harsh.

'No more than I will,' he said unexpectedly, and once again she caught a brief glimpse of uncertainty in his eyes.

'I thought you'd taken to the role of Lord de Mornington as to the "manor" born,' she challenged, and his smile was once more cynical, wary, dangerous, just as she remembered it.

'Oh, no, you didn't,' he corrected softly. 'You're waiting for me to fall flat on my face and reveal myself for the barbarian you really consider me to be.'

She caught her breath, hurt and indignant.

'That's both unkind and untrue!' she declared. 'How can you say such a thing, when it was I who did my utmost from the start to persuade you to come here?'

'You mean you don't consider me a barbarian?' A half-humorous smile lit the planes of his face, sharply angled in the lamplight. 'In that case, why do I sense you putting up your defences every time I come near you?'

Cordelia swallowed painfully. How could she answer that charge, without admitting the effect he had on her?

'I think there's still a lot of anger and resentment in you, and some of it, quite mistakenly, is directed against me,' she said warily.

'Mistakenly?' Gil poured the last of the champagne into their glasses. 'I was tolerably content in La Vega, until you came along. I told you how I felt, but you couldn't leave well alone. You had to write to me in glowing colours, whetting my curiosity and stirring my imagination, until I *had* to see Mornington Hall for myself.'

'Obviously you liked what you saw,' she retorted. 'Look at you—no one would believe you were the man I met in La Vega.'

'Yes, look at me,' he echoed ruefully. 'I appear convincing, don't I? Half of *me* even believes in Gillan de Mornington! But only half. I no longer know where I belong. Yet I've acquired a whole new set of responsibilities. People depend on me. I'm involved here. I'm not free any more.'

He set the glass down almost savagely, and Cordelia trembled at the strength of suppressed emotion in him. She realised that he was *not* acting a part—he *was* two people at the same time, and wholly comfortable with neither of them. Why had she not understood how difficult and painful the transition would be?

'I'm sorry, Gil,' she said quietly, shaken by a fierce current of feelings she had never expected to experience in regard to him—compassion, remorse, empathy with his dilemma. 'I truly didn't realise what I was doing.'

Somehow, just the admission of regret loosened the tension in him, and he smiled jauntily.

'I shouldn't be blaming you. Perhaps I never was free—merely clinging to the illusion of it. Finish your drink, and I'll walk you home.'

She was oddly reluctant to leave the bright spotlight of his attention. While they sat in the glowing circle of warmth and comfort, alone and yet safe against a background of reassuring human activity, there had been a subtle shift in their dealings with one another. Gil Montero—confident, ruthless, assured—had actually dared to admit he had doubts and uncertainties, and she, instead of sparring with him as an adversary, had given in to a rush of sympathy. She wanted to hold that moment, but she knew it could not last. She wanted to trust him, to surrender to her growing attraction to him, but she dared not risk it.

The streets were quiet now, as they walked back to the shop. Cordelia expected him to leave her there, but he insisted on escorting her down the narrow alley to the back entrance, and waiting as she unlocked the door.

'Thank you for the drink,' she said. 'I hadn't expected it to be champagne!'

'Does this farewell mean you aren't going to ask me in?' he said, smiling a little.

She shook her head.

'I really am tired, Gil.'

'No, you aren't,' he contradicted calmly. 'You're scared. But there's no need to be. I don't make advances to women unless they want me to.'

Cordelia gave a short laugh.

'The trouble with you, Gil, is that you *assume* all women want you to, even when they plainly tell you otherwise. So I think I'd better say goodnight now.'

He shrugged. 'Even though that isn't really what you want to do?'

What she *wanted*? Cordelia hardly knew how to express what she wanted. She did not have words to describe how she felt about him, and nothing she had ever experienced in the past gave her any guidance as to how to deal with those feelings. He was right—she *was* scared. Not that he would try to make love to her against her wishes, but that she actively desired him to, and would not have the power to say no.

'Let's not continue with this any further,' she said. 'Have a lovely Christmas. And I hope... I hope you manage to work it all out for the best.'

Tentatively, involuntarily, her hand reached up, impelled by a deep if unconscious need to touch him, and her fingers very lightly brushed his cheek. His reaction was like lightning, so swift and instinctive she had no chance of forestalling it. He grasped her hand, turned it over, and pressed his mouth to the palm, burning her cool skin with its warmth, then almost in the same movement, his other arm snaked around her waist, gathering her tightly to him. Releasing her fingers, he cupped the back of her head in his hand, tangling it in the mass of her hair so that her chin came up, her head tipped back, and she had no way of escaping his mouth.

His kiss was relentlessly thorough, devouring her with an almost savage hunger. There seemed to be no breath in her lungs, no chance to inhale—it was like being dragged beneath a powerful wave, and yet there was a fierce exhilaration in her very helplessness. She gasped for air as his mouth moved to her throat, her hands clutched at the lapels of his jacket, and irresistibly slid around his neck, and into the thick dark hair at the nape.

She felt herself being expertly and inexorably propelled into the hall, the darkened stairway to her flat loomed ahead, but this was a hurdle Gil would take swiftly in his stride, as were the layers of winter clothing they were both wearing. The momentum was carrying her forward to a point where neither he nor she would be able to retreat. His raw strength frightened her, even as a part of her longed to be overcome by it. An hour from now, what would she be? Another victim, about whom he could smile reminiscently now and then, or forget—as *he* chose.

She tensed her hands against his chest, struggling to free herself from his commanding grip.

'Gil, stop it! What are you doing?'

His laugh was softly contemptuous.

'I'm taking you upstairs, to your bedroom, wherever that may be. Groping in doorways is for teenagers,' he said purposefully. 'I want to make love to you properly—memorably. Stop holding out, Cordelia! You know you want it too!'

She reached up desperately for the electric switch, flooding the hall with light. The stark, determined desire in his eyes devastated her anew, causing her to tremble with fear and need. This was a practised seducer, not a callow boy who would allow her to lead him on, then back away. She either stopped now, or let him go ahead and do exactly as he pleased with her.

'You don't keep your word, do you, Gil?' she demanded, her breath coming roughly, unevenly. 'You said—you said you wouldn't touch me unless I invited you to.'

'Ah, but you did,' he said. His own breathing was under control now, although his eyes were still dark with arousal, and his body so taut, so ready for attack, that she dared not move. 'You touched *me* first, remember? That was an invitation if ever I saw one, or so I interpreted it. It isn't always what women say, Cordelia. It's their eyes, their bodies. Yours were begging me to get on with it! You're either a tease, or a virgin, or both!'

She flushed at the all too accurate mockery in his voice.

'I'm *not* a tease, and as for the other, that's none of your business!' she exclaimed.

'It very nearly was, though, wouldn't you say?' he demanded softly. 'A word of warning, *chica*. Before we get into this situation again, be very sure where you want it to end. I held back this time. I won't be prepared to do so the next.'

Cordelia's cheeks were stinging with shame.

'There won't be a next time!' she whispered fiercely.

He stood absolutely still, looking down at her with thoughtful consideration, a small, aloof smile creasing the corner of his mouth. Dark, grave and desirable— she wanted to flail at him with her fists, but did not dare, because she knew, beyond a shadow, that any contact between them, of any kind, right now, could have only one end.

'Oh, yes, there will,' he said dispassionately, stating it as a matter of fact, quite impersonally, as if he were discussing something quite mundane, not the most intimate activity in which a man and woman could engage. 'You will come to me one day, Cordelia, of your own free will, ready to give. Indeed, eager to give. I know it.'

He shrugged.

'Whether I shall then want you is a chance you will have to take,' he went on remorselessly, in the same level, unconcerned voice. 'Until then——' His shoulders rose again suggestively.

Cordelia shook her head fiercely, denying any vestige of truth in his prophecy, even as her whole self cried out for him.

'You *are* a barbarian!' she spat at him furiously. 'I'd begun to give you the benefit of the doubt, to think that just perhaps there was some good in you! Thank you very much for reminding me that I was right all along!'

His smile did not falter, and the mockery in his eyes was unabashed.

'*No hay de qué,*' he said with scathing unconcern. 'Don't mention it.'

CHAPTER SEVEN

AT THE end, Christmas proved to be, although not white, in the sense that it did not snow, bright and sparkly, with clear, cold, star-filled nights and frosty mornings. Cordelia went to a small party given by friends on Christmas Eve, but, as she had planned, spent the actual day alone.

In reality, she was spending it with the beloved memory of her father, doing on her own the things they would have done together. She cooked a *poussin*—anything else would have been silly, for one, but she served it nicely with fresh greens and roast potato, the table properly set, and a half-bottle of wine. She opened presents and listened to the Queen's speech, and fell asleep in front of the television watching a film she was sure they trotted out every year, since she could almost recite the dialogue. She was saying goodbye, letting go, acknowledging that the future would be different.

In one way, it already was, for there was an intruder at the feast. Gil Montero, although she had not invited him, would not set her free. His mocking voice kept invading her thoughts. She saw his eyes, his face, at odd moments when she had just persuaded herself she had finally banished him.

'You will come to me one day, of your own free will...' To offer herself? To plead with him to take her, and make her his? To be another of his occasional and briefly-remembered women? *No!* she vowed fervently. How amused he would be to know she was being so endlessly plagued and troubled by these thoughts. She could

115

almost hear his laughter... *'No hay de qué...'* Strange how he lapsed into Spanish at such moments...

She poured herself a large brandy and went to bed with a book of Gustav Klimt drawings Bryce had given her. Considering her mood, and on top of the wine she had already drunk, the brandy was foolish and superfluous, and she awoke on Boxing Day with a thick head, the remedy for which, she decided sternly, was a brisk walk along the footpath which ran beside the river.

In former days she would have taken her sketchbook along. As it was, she excused herself that it was cold, and difficult to sketch with gloved hands. She had done no drawing since she came back from Spain last summer, and certainly had not touched a paintbrush. Walking quickly to combat the chill in the air, she reasoned that she had anyhow been far too busy, especially with the coffee shop to launch, but she could not fool herself that this was the entire truth.

The sketches she had done in La Vega were good, she knew, but she could not bear to look at them. The creative urge was still locked up tight within her, unable to rediscover the brief renaissance which had fuelled it that summer morning—the same morning that had found her struggling in Gil Montero's arms, fighting another urge, equally fierce, and strongly suppressed.

Art and sensuality. Were they somehow yoked together in her now, like two horses reined to the same carriage, who could not pull together, and yet were useless apart? She tried to shake off this uncomfortable suspicion, but she knew that Gil had awoken something in her which needed to find expression. Oh, but *why* did it so perversely ache to find it with him? She had never specifically thought of herself as a sensual person, although she knew it was her nature to respond to colour, texture and form. Was it a part of that same impulse, this need to be kissed and touched, to be seized and overcome by sensation?

Was she, she wondered unhappily, one of those women one heard about, who became disastrously obsessed with one man—a man whom they could not have, or who could not love them, and would only cause them pain and humiliation? She had aroused Gil's desire—at least, when she was with him, he had desired her; probably he felt that casual need for any number of women, to whom he never gave a thought when they were out of his sight. And even for this small reward, he expected her virtually to throw herself at him! No—and no again!

She arrived back at the flat with her head clear, but no happier in her mind. She had walked for so long that it was too late for breakfast, and too early for lunch, and she was just toying with the idea of making a cup of coffee when the telephone rang.

It was Gaynor, and she sounded agitated.

'Cordelia, I have to see you. It's important,' she said urgently.

'Gaynor? What's wrong?' Cordelia asked, wondering what crisis could be taking place at Mornington Hall, for Gil's sister to be phoning her on Boxing Day.

'I can't speak—not over the phone,' Gaynor insisted. 'Can you meet me?'

'Of course, if it's that vital,' Cordelia said worriedly. 'Tell me where, and I'll come at once. Are you at home?'

'Yes. You know the main gate to the Hall? I'll wait for you there.'

Gaynor rang off before Cordelia could enquire further. Frowning, she pulled on her warm sweater over her tan cords and brushed cotton shirt, slipped on her jacket, and locking the flat, went to get her car from the nearby garage where she kept it.

All the way out she puzzled over what might be troubling Gaynor. She had grown quite fond of the girl, who had slaved happily in the coffee shop every day for a week, refusing to accept any recompense other than the odd free cream cake, and she could not refuse now, if Gaynor needed her help.

Gaynor's bright red Mini Cooper was parked outside the gates of Mornington Hall when she arrived, and she could see the girl slumped inside it, head bent over the steering-wheel. She appeared to be in considerable distress, and jumping out of her own car, Cordelia ran across, wrenched open the door of the Mini, and slid into the passenger seat.

'Gaynor, please don't cry,' she urged. 'Tell me what's the matter.'

The transformation was incredible. Gaynor sat up, and she was not crying at all, but grinning ear to ear, a hitherto unknown sparkle in her eyes as she turned the key in the ignition, and the engine sprang to life.

The abrupt take-off flung Cordelia back in her seat.

'Would you mind telling me what's going on?' she cried, as the car rocketed off up the long drive.

'Don't even ask!' Gaynor shouted back. 'Belt up—literally—and hold on for your life!'

It was good advice, as she did the drive to Mornington Hall, meant for a stately prowl, at sixty miles an hour. Cordelia could say little above the noise of the engine, but an awful, angry suspicion was beginning to grow inside her, and as they drew up outside the house, it hardened to a furious certainty. For there, standing on the neatly gravelled forecourt, with the two Afghans posed beautifully beside him, was the lord of the manor himself, better known to her as Gil Montero, and his expression was smug to the point of triumph.

Cordelia leapt out, hands clenched, shivering with outrage.

'I,' she declared in haughty disgust, 'have just been kidnapped! Correct me if I'm wrong, but I assume that *you* are the perpetrator!'

'You're not wrong,' he said unashamedly. 'Come on in—we're just about to have a buffet lunch.'

Cordelia glared from one to the other of them.

'Of all the underhand——' she exploded. 'Gaynor, I'm surprised at you, although nothing *he* did——' she nodded curtly in Gil's direction '—could possibly shock me any more!'

Gaynor bit her lip, clearly taken aback by the strength of Cordelia's reaction to what, to her, was simply an amusing prank, and Gil slipped an arm protectively around her thin shoulders.

'You mustn't blame Gaynor. The idea and the strategy were entirely mine,' he said. 'I persuaded her you'd see the funny side of it.'

'But I wanted you to come too,' Gaynor said eagerly. 'Gil said he'd asked you for Christmas, and that you wouldn't, because you thought it would be an intrusion. It isn't—there are heaps of people in there.'

Cordelia sighed exasperatedly. It was a long, cold walk back to where she had left her car, and her initial annoyance was tempered by the memory of Gaynor's laughing face as she drove off, and Gil's swift, instinctive leap to his sister's defence. That had to count for something.

'Very well,' she capitulated. 'But it's most unfair of you both! I'm not dressed for visiting. Heavens, I haven't even got any make-up on!'

'You can borrow some of mine, and as for dress, everyone is very casual,' Gaynor declared. Indeed, she herself was in trousers and the sweater Cordelia had given her, which was a perfect match for her eyes, and emphasised her delicately rose-pale skin.

'Go along,' Gil ordered easily. 'You look fine to me, but go and do whatever you women do to your faces, and I'll see you both later, in the drawing-room.'

He turned, waving an airy hand, and strode inside, the dogs slouching faithfully after him. What was it, Cordelia wondered, about Gil Montero and animals? He seemed to have an effortless rapport with them.

'I couldn't resist,' Gaynor confessed when they were in her bedroom, Cordelia contenting herself with a slick of coral lipstick and a squirt of Anaïs Anaïs. 'I did want you to be here, because you're my friend, and besides, I knew it would make Alyssa as sick as a pig. You can call me mean if you like, but that gives me a certain satisfaction!'

Cordelia turned sharply, comb in hand.

'Why should it matter to Alyssa if I'm here?' she asked, frowning, and Gaynor giggled with unaffected pleasure.

'Because she thinks you fancy Gil, silly, and she suspects it might be mutual,' she explained with patent glee.

'That's nonsense!' Cordelia said briskly, hoping she sounded convincing.

'You wouldn't be alone—he does seem to have a certain effect on women,' Gaynor observed. 'And he did go to all this trouble and subterfuge to inveigle you into coming to Mornington Hall.'

'He just enjoys having his own way, and takes it as a personal affront if anyone refuses him anything,' Cordelia argued. 'I don't mean anything special to him, I can assure you.'

'Nor he to you?'

This girl was getting altogether too sharp, Cordelia thought, as she said, 'I have a business to run. I don't have time for romance.' And she hoped that would be an end to an uncomfortable subject.

The long drawing-room was, as Gaynor had intimated, full of people—in fact, they overflowed out into
the hall. Cordelia did not know any of them personally,
although she recognised several faces from the social
pages of *Country Life*. The county set—people who
owned land, who rode with hounds and attended hunt
balls, men in tweeds whose wives did voluntary charity
work, whose sons attended good public schools, and
whose daughters were 'finished' in France.

Gil took her arm, gave her a drink, and casually introduced her around, then he led her into the dining-
room, where the buffet was spread out invitingly.

'Enjoying yourself?' he asked wickedly, and she bared
her teeth at him in a parody of a smile.

'I feel like a fish left on the beach when the tide has
gone out! You must realise that I don't know any of
these people. I can imagine them all thinking, who on
earth is she, and what's she doing here?'

'That's ridiculous, Cordelia,' he said impatiently. 'I
have only the merest acquaintance with many of them,
myself—they're Evelyn's friends, but people are people.
They all laugh, cry, give birth, make love.' His sidelong
glance mocked her slightly. 'If I can adapt, anyone can.
I may be different, but *no one* is going to make me feel
inferior.'

She looked down at the table, groaning beneath the
huge cuts of cold beef, turkey and ham, and a whole
salmon dressed in aspic and decorated with sliced cu-
cumber and red pepper.

'But you weren't lured here under false pretences, and
against your will!' she protested.

'Was I not?' he challenged softly, and her red curls
danced angrily as she shook her head.

'You know what I mean! You shouldn't have deceived
me the way you did.'

'It worked, didn't it?' he retorted, smiling complacently. 'I told you I usually got what I wanted.'

'You didn't. I wasn't here for Christmas,' she pointed out.

'Not for Christmas Day, but then I figured you might have good reasons for being at home on that day,' he said. 'I respected them. I could easily have got Gaynor to pull that trick yesterday—and you would have come, wouldn't you? Your own generous nature wouldn't have allowed you to refuse.'

He imprisoned her gaze with his, and she could not deny the force of his argument. She had firmly and categorically refused to spend time at Mornington Hall, but there she was, because *he* had decreed that she should be. And yes, it would have made no difference had Gaynor's telephone call disturbed her yesterday. She would have come.

'You have no compunction about taking advantage of my "generous nature", then?' she accused.

'None whatsoever. When I want to prove a point, I'll use any method that comes to hand.'

A terrible weakness afflicted all her limbs, making it impossible for her to walk away from him, as she would have liked to do. The power she had felt emanating from him, the first day they met, in La Vega, was once again threatening to engulf her. Two fierce, conflicting forces were using her as a battlefield—a need to fight him, and an equally seductive desire to give in.

'What—what point is that?' she asked faintly.

'That you're fighting a rising ride,' he said. 'Let me know when you finally acknowledge the futility of it.'

And then she did turn, desperate to escape, breaking away from him and politely but urgently threading her way through little knots of people standing around talking and drinking. But somehow, instead of ending up in the hall, she took the wrong door, and found herself in a long conservatory, full of tall ferns and trailing greenery, trees in tubs, terracotta pots of unseasonal flowering plants, and secluded little groups of cane chairs and sofas.

A soft, husky laugh made her realise she was not alone here, and then she heard Alyssa's voice say cuttingly, 'Don't be silly, Sebastian—I told you, I'm not going to the New Year Ball with you.'

'But you promised!' The young man's voice was petulant with disappointment. 'I say, Alyssa, that's not fair!'

'I certainly didn't promise *anything*,' she snapped. 'Anyhow, it's all arranged. I'm going with my cousin Gil.'

Cordelia would have slipped back the way she had come, but just then the enraged Sebastian stalked off in a huff, and she almost had to jump out of his way.

Alyssa's silvery-blonde head appeared round a parlour palm, and then the rest of her, slim and willowy in a burgundy velvet catsuit.

'Oh, it's only you, Cordelia,' she said with a dismissive shrug. 'I suppose you heard that, but no matter. Boys are so irritating, aren't they—give me a mature man any day! I'm sure *you* agree.'

The hint of complicity in her smile made Cordelia's already ragged nerves jump disconcertingly.

'I don't have the leisure to contemplate such things at great length,' she said, with forced coolness.

'Unlike me, you mean?' Alyssa's smile was gaily malicious. 'Ah, well—the pleasures of being a social butterfly, you know!'

She plucked a frond of fern, and with idle fingers began carelessly shredding it to bits.

'Actually, I do more...ah...contemplating...than anything else, when it comes to men,' she murmured wickedly. 'Contrary to whatever dear Gaynor might have indicated...well, she's a bit naïve, you know? I might flirt a lot, but I don't sleep around.'

'I'm sure it's none of my business,' said Cordelia, her spine stiffening, wishing desperately that she were not involved in this conversation.

'It certainly isn't!' Alyssa's tone had changed; it was cold and knife-sharp, without even a pretence of friend-liness. 'Imagine, if you can, what it's been like, growing up here as a poor relation. I've no money of my own, you know. Aunt Evelyn gives me an allowance, but most of that has to be spent on clothes—well, you know what a price *decent* things are these days.'

Her green eyes scanned Cordelia swiftly and critically as she stressed the word 'decent', as if to say that most likely Cordelia would have no idea of the cost of de-signer outfits.

'Uncle Giles has left me something, if the estate ever gets sorted out, but most of that is craftily tied up in trusts, so that I can't get my naughty little hands on it until I'm old and grey!'

Unable to escape, Cordelia helplessly watched the pieces of fern drifting down to fall, spent, on the grey and white travertine marble floor. She would have given five years of her life, at that moment, for some magic to spirit her away from Alyssa's light but carefully focused malice.

'I'm sure it's hard for you,' she could not help mur-muring, with faint sarcasm.

'Very hard, but it won't be forever.' Alyssa's laugh was harsh, and suddenly, all the features which had seemed so delicate and lovely were hard. 'There's hope, now that Gil's here. He's my way out. Someone has to be the next Lady de Mornington, and who is better qualified for the position than I am?'

Cordelia forced a smile. The whole scene was so bizarre, she almost believed she must be dreaming it.

'I wouldn't imagine Gil to be interested in marriage,' she said.

'Oh, probably not,' Alyssa agreed. 'He'd rather just get me into bed, because that's the kind of man he is, and he's used to having things his way. But I'm playing for higher stakes. He'll have to marry eventually, but in the meantime, if he chooses to amuse himself, I can hardly complain, can I?'

She shrugged unconcernedly, still smiling, and a hot red tide of angry embarrassment washed over Cordelia as it dawned on her what the other girl meant. She, Cordelia, was the amusement, the equivalent of a little shop girl or actress or whatever, with whom Gil's ancestors were wont to pass the time until they settled down with a suitable marriage partner—and perhaps even afterwards! She had never in her life felt so soiled, so sordid, so utterly degraded, because crazy as it was, a nagging, unsavoury suspicion lurking at the back of her mind insisted that somewhere in all this there might just be a grain of truth.

Gil Montero was now Lord de Mornington, and appeared to have accepted that fact, whatever private reservations he had about it. Unless he wanted to cause legal chaos for the estate in years to come, he needed a legitimate heir. And here was his spiteful chit of a cousin telling her, in effect, that men in Gil's position might amuse themselves with girls like Cordelia, but they married girls like Alyssa.

Somehow—how, she never understood—Cordelia kept her cool. She even managed a frosty little smile, as if to disclaim all interest in where or with whom Gil slept, and whom he eventually married.

'I'm sure I wish you joy of each other,' she said nonchalantly. 'I think you're perfectly suited. Now, if you'll excuse me...'

She turned and walked out of the conservatory without looking back, but Alyssa's soft, triumphant laughter followed her, and echoed in her ears.

In the drawing-room, the party was still going on. People were eating from heaped plates, their glasses were being refilled, they were carefree, festive, laughing. Only Cordelia felt as if she had been wrung out emotionally, for in those few short minutes since she left the room Alyssa had shown her—as she surely meant to—her own very lowly place in this elevated world.

'Ah, there you are, Cordelia.' Lady Mornington materialised at her side, a faint frown on her smooth brow. 'My dear, are you sure you're well? You look positively white!'

Cordelia was about to grasp thankfully at this excuse to leave, and declare that she did not feel well at all, which was true—she felt sick and shaken. But she did not get the chance, for Gil had already spotted her, and was making his way purposefully across the room.

Taking her arm in a firm grip, he smiled and said, 'I think Cordelia's probably only suffering from hunger pangs, Evelyn. She hasn't eaten a thing since she arrived.'

Actually, since she had missed breakfast, Cordelia had not eaten all day, but she was sure that in spite of her empty stomach she could not face food now.

'I'm not hungry,' she said stubbornly.

'Nonsense,' he replied with equal obstinacy, propelling her into the drawing-room. 'You must have something. The Coronation chicken is very good. And how about some smoked trout...'

He piled her plate with food, then found her somewhere to sit—the perfect, attentive host. Cordelia pushed her fork listlessly around her plate, pecking at the odd mouthful with difficulty, but he was not deceived.

'What's wrong?' he demanded, planting himself on the chair next to hers. He was so close she was overcome by the warm, clean male aroma of him, faint with a need she knew she could never satisfy.

'Nothing.' She shook her head weakly. There was no way she could ever tell him about that unpleasant little scene with Alyssa.

'Oh, come on—do you seriously expect me to believe that? Something's bothering you. Where did you disappear to when you ran away from me?'

She flinched.

'I did *not* run away. I found the turn of the conversation distasteful, and I needed some fresh air. I was in the conservatory.'

'Distasteful?' He mulled over the word, a thoughtful smile playing around his lips. 'You don't like the truth? We're attracted to one another—violently. It's not new. I wanted you the first day you walked into my house in La Vega, and whatever you say, I know you feel the same. That's not conceit, it's plain fact. When are you going to do something about it?'

Like warming your bed until you get tired of me? she thought bitterly. Letting you use me and then cast me to one side?

'I don't want to get involved with you, Gil,' she said.

He gave a contemptuous snort.

'You don't want to get involved with life, in a real sense, at all,' he said. 'How long are you going to use your father's death as an excuse for sealing yourself away like an exhibit in a glass case? Is *that* what he would want for you? Start living, Cordelia. Who knows, you might even start painting again.'

'I don't have to put up with this!' she exclaimed, her voice low but agitated. 'What gives you the right to lecture me?'

'The same concern that gave *you* the right to preach to *me* about my responsibilities, back in La Vega,' he replied implacably. 'I'm merely returning the compliment. Climb out of the case, Cordelia.'

She made as if to stand up, but he laid a peremptory hand on her knee, forestalling her, so that she could not jerk away without causing a scene which would attract the attention of others in the room. And again, as always, the pressure of his fingers sent tremors of delight and apprehension coursing through her.

'Let me go!' she whispered urgently. 'I want to go home.'

He kept his hand there for a full minute, his eyes locking hard into hers, demanding submission. She returned his stare, forcing herself not to give way, remaining still, enduring his touch, fighting not to betray the excitement mounting to an unbearable fever pitch inside her. Only the presence of other people prevented him from running his fingers up her thigh, but she felt the intensity of his desire to do so as a palpable force, and the mere thought sent an erotic charge through her, which she could barely contain. When at last he removed his hand she was weak with reaction.

'Give me your car keys,' he said calmly.

'Why?' She could not even think clearly or speak sensibly. Even to herself, her voice sounded dazed and stupid.

'It's a long walk to where you parked the car,' he replied patiently. 'I'll have someone bring it to the door for you.'

Then he left her, and she watched him circulating unconcernedly among his guests, joining in conversations here and there, his laugh ringing out, his arm casually resting around the shoulders of an extremely pretty girl.

So much for his violent attraction, his insatiable need for her! He appeared to have forgotten about it already.

Alyssa was right. Somewhere in this room was the sort of girl who would one day be Lady de Mornington, and she would probably have been bred to turn a blind eye to her husband's roving lust and constant philandering.

He paid no more attention to Cordelia after that, and it was Lady de Mornington who saw her out, thanked her for coming, and wished her the very best for the New Year ahead.

Cordelia returned her good wishes sincerely. She sensed a warm and compassionate nature behind Gil's stepmother's cool and reserved exterior.

'I think it will be a good year,' she said hopefully. 'Of course, I still miss Giles, and always will, but at least the estate is back on an even keel, now Gil is here. Dearly as I love Ran, I have to admit he wouldn't make half so good a job of running things. I do hope Gil decides to stay.'

'Is there still some doubt about that?' Cordelia could not resist asking.

'Well, yes.' Evelyn de Mornington frowned. 'The fact of being Lord de Mornington doesn't mean he's obliged to live here, although obviously it's better for the estate if he does. I worry that, although he doesn't speak of it much, part of his heart is still in Spain.'

I wish the rest of him had stayed there, Cordelia thought bitterly as she drove home. I wish I'd never meddled, never had the temerity to persuade him to come to England.

Maybe he would have come anyhow, impelled by an inescapable curiosity to seek out this other half of himself. But she need not have been involved. They need never have been brought together, and she would have had only the memory of a man she had met briefly, in a strange place, who had attracted her for a short while. It need have gone no further than that.

Instead, she had found herself drawn into the circle of people and events surrounding him, and with every meeting his power over her had grown stronger. So that now, whatever happened, even if she walked away from him and avoided all further contact, she had passed the point where she could tear him out of her dreams and out of her heart. She was falling in love with him, and she had never intended that to happen!

CHAPTER EIGHT

WHEREVER Cordelia happened to look, that winter, she could not escape from images of Gil. The local Press carried photographs of the new Lord de Mornington opening a factory, there were reports of speeches he had given to this or that society, after a dinner or luncheon. Glossy magazines which specialised in the doings of the country set depicted him dancing with various titled young women, heiresses to proud names and great fortunes. He was deeply involved with charities concerning wildlife and conservation, and gave generously of his time and energy, she learned. Meanwhile, gossip columns in the dailies began to speculate about the romantic liaisons and marriage plans of this dashing new member of the aristocracy.

He had taken to it all like a duck to water, she thought, at least on the surface. After all, it was in his blood, and one did not have to search too deeply to reveal what had been there, all along, dormant and waiting to come to life.

But from what Lady de Mornington had said to her on Boxing Day, from the occasional wry comment Gil himself had let slip, and the odd, wistful look in the flint-dark eyes, Cordelia could not help wondering if he still felt vaguely like an outsider—if the life he had left behind did not still tug at his heart, now and then. If so, he concealed it so well that few would have guessed.

She saw him herself occasionally—mostly from a distance. Once, in Hereford's High Town, where the traffic crawled slowly round the one-way system circling the historic centre, he passed her, driving a sleek, shining car. In the passenger seat beside him was Alyssa, wearing a coat with a white fur collar that made her look like a fairy princess. The smirk on her face as she caught sight of Cordelia was heavy with triumph, but if Gil saw her at all, he gave no sign of it.

She got a glimpse of him at the races, field-glasses around his neck, deep in conversation with Ranulf, and at a choral concert in the Cathedral there he was again, seated among the city's dignitaries. This time he spared her an aloof smile as their eyes met briefly across the heads of others, but he turned his attention at once back to the music, and did not look in her direction again.

Cordelia felt her heart splinter painfully in her chest, and for a few moments it actually hurt her to breathe. She had not believed hearts really could physically experience pain in that way, but now she knew it was so. How had it happened that she had come to love this man who had moved into a world far from her own, although their lives ran parallel? Gil had never pretended that he loved her, or given her any indication that he considered it a possibility that he might.

All he had wanted was to take her to bed. All he had offered her was the bitter joy of being, fleetingly, the object of his desire. He certainly had not wanted her love, and would probably have considered it an embarrassing burden. She had always suspected that he lacked the capability to give which loving required, but that did not console her very much. She wanted to be the one to help him find that ability in himself, and it hurt her that she apparently could not.

There could be no greater happiness than being that unique and special person for the one you loved, she imagined, but it seemed that happiness was not for her.

She threw herself into trying to make a success of her business, and tried hard, if vainly, not to let her longing dreams stray to Gil too often. And still her paintbrushes lay idle.

She had seen nothing of him, not even a distant glimpse for some weeks, when on a day when spring seemed just around the corner, she all but ran slap into him, coming through the Cathedral Close.

He caught her shoulders and set her straight, and her nerves began to sing their familiar refrain of desire and anxiety as she looked up into his gravely smiling but dispassionate face. She had been shopping for food, and as often happened, the few intended purchases had become a lot more as she browsed the supermarket shelves, so that she now had a plastic bag of groceries in each hand. Gil took the heavier one from her, without giving her a chance to protest.

'The weights you women attempt to carry!' he said mildly. 'Why on earth didn't you take your car?'

'It just developed—I found lots of things I realised I needed,' she retorted defensively.

'What? You mean you actually need all this stuff, right now—today? What are you having, a dinner party for twenty?'

'And if I am, I don't have the devoted Simpson and his minions to help out,' she remarked.

He gave a lofty grin.

'You only have to say—I'll lend him to you,' he offered, and the notion of the dignified de Mornington butler announcing 'Dinner is served' in her minute flat was too much for Cordelia. A glimmer of humour appeared in her blue eyes, despite her thumping, despairing heart, and her frighteningly erratic pulse.

'Pass,' she said ruefully, and then, 'It's been...it's been some time, Gil. Have you been away?'

'In London,' he told her sagely. 'Taking my seat in the House of Lords.'

A peal of sardonic laughter escaped her, and an all too familiar expression on his face hinted that he only half believed it himself.

'Yes, this savage is a peer of the realm,' he said darkly. 'What *is* the world coming to? I hear you say.'

Cordelia picked up the dangerous, challenging note in his voice.

'As a matter of fact, I was merely wondering if our illustrious Upper House was ready for you,' she said lightly.

He fell into step beside her as they strode down Church Street.

'Why not? I behaved myself impeccably,' he said, and she could not tell if he were serious or mocking. 'New boys are expected to keep quiet for some time, you know, so that's precisely what I did.'

'I find it hard to imagine,' she sniffed.

'You *would* find it hard to imagine, Cordelia—the whole experience,' he said, and now there was no doubting the gravity in his voice. 'All that historic ceremonial, the famous faces and the famous names, the almost overpowering weight of tradition. It's very impressive. I felt a need to pinch myself from time to time, to make sure it was real.'

Six months ago he had been a dispossessed outcast, living in a rural mountain village in a remote part of Spain. Now he sat among the ranks of the great, as his ancestors had done. The magnitude of the change he had undergone, and taken superbly in his stride, swept over Cordelia anew. No wonder there was no real place for her in his new life.

'Oh, I'm sure you'll soon get accustomed to it,' she said in a tight little voice. 'I read that a well-known gossip columnist has been making wagers on your marriage prospects.'

Gil laughed. 'I read that too.'

'Doesn't it annoy you?' She was piqued by the equanimity and tolerance of his reaction.

'Why should it? These people have a living to earn,' he said, with a familiar and very Hispanic shrug. 'Some day, as Evelyn keeps hinting, I suppose I shall have to oblige them, for the good of the family and the estate.'

She listened hard for a note of facetious mockery in his voice, but did not hear it, and had to conclude that he was perfectly serious.

'Just like that? It doesn't really matter who she is?' she asked incredulously.

'Well, of course it matters, my dear Cordelia,' he said equably. 'You know that Ran is into show-jumping? I'm encouraging him to breed horses for the ring, to turn a hobby into something both satisfying and profitable. We're talking bloodlines here. If you want to breed a winner, it doesn't happen by chance.'

'But that's *horses*, Gil!' she protested, shocked. 'You, in spite of your proclivities, are a human being, not a prize stallion! Doesn't love come into it anywhere along the line?'

'I'm not sure I know what love is, Cordelia,' he said thoughtfully. 'I'm not sure I want to. It didn't do my mother any good, did it? As I see it, there's desire, which is natural, and there's marriage, which is to do with society and property. I don't see that love need enter into either, and I'd rather tell a woman honestly what it is I want of her, than fill her head with romantic claptrap.'

They had reached her door by now, and Cordelia, fitting her key in the lock with hands that struggled to remain steady, said, 'That's certainly blunt enough.'

'I told you I was pretty basic,' Gil said practically. 'The trappings I wore in the House, and the de Mornington legacy, can't alter the way I am inside. The way I feel...or am unable to feel.'

Inside Cordelia, a leaden weight of misery and hope-lessness settled in a place from which she knew she would never entirely dislodge it. She loved the wrong man—but how could she help herself? She wanted the feel of his arms around her, his mouth on hers, even though he had told her plainly enough it meant nothing more than sex to him.

He insisted on carrying her bag up the stairs to the landing.

'There you are. In future, don't try to carry so much at once, unless you want to end up with arms like King Kong,' he advised, setting it down on the floor. 'That would be a pity, since the rest of you is in such perfect proportion.'

She hoped that the dimness of the landing hid her blush. How silly to feel like a green schoolgirl, simply because Gil paid her a casual compliment. How awful, too, that she did not want to let him go now, not knowing when, or if ever, she would see him or talk to him alone like this again.

'Would you…er…like a coffee or anything?' she asked diffidently.

'That would depend on what's included in "anything",' he said softly. 'If you ask me in, Cordelia, I know, as you do, that I shall want to make love to you. So unless that's your intention too…'

'Can't you be with a woman on any other terms?' she cried desperately. 'Isn't there such a thing as friendship in your book?'

'Yes, there is,' he agreed. 'Maybe we could be friends, but we would have to be lovers first. This feeling…this need, is in our way. We can't do or be anything until we settle it between us. When I'm with you, I'm obsessed with wanting you. It's all or nothing.'

He did not touch her, but his eyes travelled slowly over her, from the tousled red curls, the flushed face, down the length of her body, all the way to her feet and back again. The scrutiny was very nearly as erotic as the caress they were both imagining, and Cordelia was aware of every nerve in her tingling with anticipation.

It would have been so easy for her, at that moment, to open her door and let him in. To give him what he wanted, now, and pray that later he would come to love her for herself. She was not so naïve that she did not realise that sometimes that was the way it happened.

Only she didn't believe it would ever be that way, with Gil. Inexperienced as she was, she didn't even think she had the sexual expertise to hold his interest for very long. As for the chances of his falling in love with *her*, of all people, when he had stated firmly enough that love was an emotion alien and unknown to him—forget it. He would break her, and she did not think she would ever recover from it.

'Then it will have to be nothing, I'm afraid,' she said, trying to sound unconcerned. 'I'm not into sex for its own sake.'

'Are you not?' he said dangerously, pulling her into his arms, not roughly, but insistently. Bending his head, he found a spot where her ear met the delicate line of her jaw, and pressed his mouth to it, exploring gently, while his hand unfastened the buttons of her jacket and slipped inside to enclose one breast. Cordelia shuddered, and her body arched obediently in response. She wanted the full weight of him against her, touching everywhere—there could never be too much, once they set out together on this road.

But she knew she also needed much more than this. She wanted to be able to look into his eyes and know she was the only woman for him, to be the one he turned to when he was sad or exultant, the one who shared all his emotions. To be his lover—yes, marvellous, wonderful, but, far beyond that, she wanted to be his love.

'Tell me to go now, Cordelia,' he murmured challengingly into her ear. 'Go ahead—tell me, now, when I can feel how aroused you are.'

It was the hardest thing she had ever done, when every inch of her was crying out for him, but somehow she kept her control. Turning her head away from him, she whispered, 'Please go, Gil. Go *now*. I can't take any more of this!'

He straightened up, his face registering not disappointment, nor even frustration, but an unfathomable contempt. Humiliatingly, he fastened up the buttons of her jacket as if she were a small child, or a doll.

'You're not a woman, you're a robot,' he said disgustedly. 'A pretty, mechanical automaton, with every part looking so beautiful, so perfect—but without a spark of life!'

And then he was gone.

Cordelia let herself into her flat with hands that fumbled. At first she was numb, frozen, unable to react. She put her shopping away, stacking cupboards and fridge without thinking, until, reaching up to a shelf, she dropped a bag of sugar from nerveless fingers, and it split, spilling all over her kitchen floor.

Something snapped inside her then. Crumpling down to a heap, she sat among the mess, her head bent, hands shielding her eyes. She could not cry, but dry, racking sobs shook her shoulders.

She had sent Gil away, but she felt no pride in her own virtue. Instead she was beset by doubts. Had her motives really been as pure as she had tried to convince herself, or was she merely afraid? Afraid to let go, to take risks with her life and her heart? Afraid to give freely, without the certainty of reward or reciprocation?

Once, not so very long ago, she had been a bright-spirited girl, confident one day of finding the place in the world her talent promised her. Sure, too, that one

day she would love someone and be loved, that it happened to everyone, and she was no exception. When the
time was right, love would come to her.

What had gone wrong, to turn her unsullied, hopeful
world into this bleak, sterile existence? Her father had
become ill, she had suffered with him, he had died, and
for a year she had shut herself away in a mental ivory
tower, living tentatively on life's surface, refusing to do
anything which might involve pain or failure. And
although she had begun, finally, to come to terms with
her grief, she had done no painting, and she had used
every excuse to avoid involvement with anyone.

Until Gil had burst into her life, awakening all her
senses... and for a while she had hovered on the brink
of flinging herself into a new world of excitement and
wonder. But she had drawn back, and she feared, now,
that there was nothing for her but the continued dullness
and emptiness of this barren plateau. The daily round
of opening the shop, existing on the edge of other
people's lives, dragging on from day to day, without
passion and without purpose.

She loved Gil, of that she was quite sure, but perhaps
he was right, and she lacked a woman's courage to
translate love into action.

'You're nothing but a robot...a pretty automaton...without a spark...' she heard his voice, withering, blasting her with its scorn. She wished fervently
that what he said were true, for then she would have no
feelings at all, and it would not hurt so much.

She did not think he would be back, not now. She
had lost the only chance she'd had, and lost it for ever.

Into the empty landscape of Cordelia's life, Bryce seemed
to slip, as if a place there was allotted to him. He took
to calling in at the shop for coffee several times during
the week, and his visits grew longer as he stopped to

chat. Cordelia neither encouraged nor discouraged him, and he took this for consent, finally becoming bold enough to suggest that he had two theatre tickets, and perhaps she might like to accompany him.

She accepted, and one outing led naturally to another, a week or so later, and then another... Cordelia found these occasions pleasant enough. Bryce behaved perfectly, and never tried to be familiar or possessive. It was only when she realised that these intermittent dates were beginning to fall into a regular pattern that she felt slightly guilty, and knew she must say something to make it clear that only friendship was on offer on her side.

So when he suggested dinner one Saturday at a well-known country inn, she laughed and said lightly, 'Bryce, perhaps you shouldn't take me out quite so often. I shall become spoiled!'

'I enjoy spoiling you, Cordelia,' he replied seriously. 'I thought you enjoyed our outings.'

She sighed.

'I do, but... Bryce, you're a single, very eligible man, and while you and I are good friends, some woman out there is probably waiting to snap you up.'

'Don't be patronising, Cordelia,' he said, quite sharply. 'Perhaps I don't want to be "snapped up", as you put it. Perhaps I'm perfectly happy taking you out on a friendly basis.'

She looked up at him, surprised, but only half believing what he had said.

'If that's so, then there's no problem,' she told him.

It was his turn to sigh.

'No, it won't do, I have to be honest,' he said. 'I would like more than friendship from you... but I'm prepared to wait until you feel ready.'

'I don't know that I shall ever feel ready,' she confessed gently. 'It's not that simple any more.'

'You mean...there's someone else?' He sounded genuinely surprised, and she sensed him trying to work out who, in the circle of people they knew, Cordelia could possibly have become involved with.

'It's someone I can't have... and who doesn't care for me,' she said quickly, and then the tightening of her lips, the determined tightening of her jaw told him firmly that was as much as she was prepared to say.

'All right, I won't push you any further on this,' he promised. 'Perhaps this...feeling...will burn itself out, given time? Meanwhile, you still need a friend, so shall I book the table?'

It would have been churlish to refuse, and Cordelia was tired of lonely dinners in her flat. The spring dusk was lengthening as the year grew, and the drive out through the verdant countryside, touched everywhere with new green, was poignantly lovely. With the right man at her side, it could have been perfect. Cordelia firmly squashed such ungrateful and pointless thoughts, and concentrated on being a pleasant companion.

The inn was fourteenth-century, black- and white-timbered, in the heart of an old village, dreaming among the cider apple orchards. Bryce and Cordelia took a table by the window, looking out over the fragrant, darkening garden, and he smiled encouragingly at her.

'Glad you came?'

'It's a lovely place,' she agreed. 'So peaceful.'

They were halfway through their main course when a party of four entered the room, and instantly Cordelia's precious feeling of ease and serenity vanished. The new arrivals were Ranulf de Mornington, accompanied by a very pretty girl with short, dark curly hair, Alyssa—and Gil.

His fine slate-blue suit made his eyes seem even darker... or maybe it was the delicate fairness of the girl clinging to his arm... Cordelia looked away, then down at her plate, but she could not control the awful temptation to look at him again, and as he followed the waiter to their table, his glance met hers.

Ranulf smiled in recognition. Alyssa did not even deign to acknowledge Cordelia, although she was sure the other girl had seen her. But Gil paused as the other three proceeded across the room.

'Cordelia. And Mr Penfold,' he said easily. His voice was quite casual and unconcerned; they were no more than acquaintances, meeting by chance, it seemed to say. But the last time she had seen him Cordelia had trembled in his arms; she remembered anew the feeling of his mouth and his hands, and a wave of helpless desire and longing swept over her.

'Hello, Gil,' she said, trying to sound calm and normally friendly. 'What a surprise—I didn't think you were a regular customer here.'

'I eat in restaurants from time to time, like everyone else,' he responded lightly. 'You'll be accusing me of slumming next!' He turned to Bryce. 'I was going to phone your office to see if you'd turned up any more of... of my father's papers in your archives.'

The hesitation was so fractional, so slight, but Cordelia noted it, and the accompanying darkness of the brow that once again emphasised the Spanish side of him.

'I'm afraid not,' Bryce replied. 'I did authorise a most diligent search, but all the de Mornington papers are now in your possession, so far as we are aware. I'm sorry we couldn't be of more help.'

Gil looked thoughtful, more puzzled than disappointed, as if something vital was narrowly eluding him.

'Not to worry. It isn't your fault,' he said with a shrug, then, 'I think I'd better join my party before they expire from starvation! Good evening.'

Cordelia tried not to watch him cross the room and take his place at the table with the other three, but her eyes could not help following him covertly. She dragged them away, and tried to concentrate on choosing her sweet course, but it was no use—her attention kept returning to its chosen subject like a hapless homing pigeon.

'You didn't tell me Gil was enquiring after some more papers,' she said, studiedly casual. 'What exactly is he looking for?'

'I don't usually discuss clients' business, Cordelia, but since he mentioned it in front of you, presumably it's no secret,' he said. 'However, I don't really know what information he's seeking. Everything is quite legal and above board, the title and all that goes with it is his beyond a doubt.'

'Something seems to be niggling him, all the same,' she mused, frowning. 'I wonder...'

'Whatever it is, he won't divulge it, and I didn't come here to talk about Gillan de Mornington,' Bryce said testily. Across the table, his eyes met Cordelia's, the latter dark with suppressed emotion, and, noting the stiff, proudly set tilt of her head, the small hands clenched on top of the white tablecloth, he groaned softly.

'So that's the way it is!' he said. 'It's him, isn't it—the man you're in love with?'

She said nothing, but her lack of denial was all the confirmation he needed. 'I think I always knew it, deep down—even in Spain, you couldn't tear yourself away from him,' he went on. 'Cordelia, don't waste your emotions! The man is a peer of the realm, and even today people like that don't marry girls they meet in the street!'

'I know that, Bryce, you don't need to remind me,' she said, tight-lipped.

'Besides, he seems very much taken with that pretty cousin of his,' he said, unwittingly but hurtfully rubbing salt in the wound. 'One sees them around together all the time.'

'Bryce, can we just drop the subject?' Cordelia begged, distress beginning to pierce her rigid control. 'In fact, can we leave, now? I really couldn't eat another thing, and I...and I...' She scrambled after her handbag which had slipped under the table, aware that unless she got out of here very quickly, she was going to disgrace herself by bursting into tears.

She knew she had brought what had begun as a pleasant evening to a bad end, and, although she apologised sincerely in the car on the way home, Bryce was not truly mollified. Cordelia in love with some anonymous, unknown individual, whom she would forget if he gave her time, he could take, but Cordelia obsessed with Gil de Mornington, who was very, very much flesh and blood, and the unfairest of competition—handsome, titled, charismatic—was far and away too much.

When he dropped her at her flat he did not, as was usual, say he would call her, or suggest another outing, and in a way Cordelia was relieved. She had felt all along that it was not quite right of her to use his affection as a prop, knowing she could hold out no hope of ever being able to return it.

Furthermore, she now had other problems to contend with, so serious that all her attention was centred on the impending and very probable failure of her business. This fear had been building up for some time, and she had resolutely kept it to herself. Christmas had been busy and profitable for the shop, but it had not made up for the months leading up to it, when she had been too involved with nursing her father to give it the necessary dedication, so that overall, the year had been a bad one.

She had taken a brave gamble opening the coffee shop, and was still convinced that, given time, it could prove a success, but as things stood now, she did not see how she could meet the repayments on the loan, keep the business afloat, and herself alive and free from insolvency.

It was the final tightening of the screw, the last, adverse straw in a scenario where everything seemed to be stacked against her. Her father had died, a lingering and unpleasant death. Her creative impulse had shrivelled within her. She was deeply and hopelessly in love with a man who could feel nothing for her but a passing lust. And now this—her livelihood was on the point of collapse.

Self-pity was a futile emotion, she told herself, struggling vainly against it, but she had no one to turn to, and it was difficult not to succumb to the overwhelming depression and a sense of hopelessness which threatened her.

It was Wednesday afternoon, early closing day, the week following her unfortunate encounter with Gil at the restaurant, and the thought of spending it closeted in her flat, trying to find some way out of her financial dilemma, filled her with despair. She needed to get out, breathe fresh air, and try, for an hour or two, to set her problems on one side, impossible as that might appear to be.

A walk around Castle Green would reassure her that the sky was still blue, birds still sang, and life went on, even though her own world was in ruins, she thought, slipping out into the street and locking the door behind her.

'Going somewhere?' said Gil's voice, behind her, and she spun round, compressing her lips and fighting to control the thumping of her heart. Oh, why did he persist in turning up, just as she was doing her best to convince herself she could live without him?

'Just to the park, for a walk,' she said. 'I'm sorry, the shop is closed.'

'I know what day it is.' Lord de Mornington wore denims—good ones, not torn and patched—and a sweater which looked like cashmere, but his casual attire was sufficient to remind her afresh of the man she had met in Spain, and something wrenched hard and painfully inside her. 'I spent the morning at the cattle market with Ran and my farm manager, learning more about the finer points of buying livestock.'

'And Alyssa?' she heard herself ask, involuntarily.

He smiled.

'Far too smelly for her,' he said, wrinkling his nose in mock disdain. 'My sister asked me to tell you she's sorry she hasn't been to see you lately. She's decided to do business studies at college next year, and she's been running around choosing the best course.'

Cordelia's face brightened temporarily.

'I'm so pleased for her—I'm sure it will be just what she needs,' she said warmly. 'But how did she know you would see me?'

'Because I expressed my intention of doing so, and I usually carry out my intentions,' he said. 'Come on, let's go to the park.'

His arrogant confidence, his assumption that he could walk in and out of her life as it suited him, enraged her.

'Did I say I wanted anyone's company—especially yours?' she flared.

'No. But you look as if you could use a strong shoulder,' he said shrewdly. 'What's wrong, Cordelia? And don't say "nothing", because I always know when you're upset or worried.'

She shrugged, and set off along the street without answering, but he fell easily into step beside her, and she could see no way of shaking him off. Nor, in her secret heart, did she really want to, for all she knew their encounters always ended badly for her.

'I don't need *your* shoulder, Gil,' she insisted doggedly.

'Whose, then? Bryce Penfold's?' They passed the entrance to the Green, once the site of the castle drawbridge, and paced along beside the bowling green. 'You've been seeing a lot of him, I gather?'

She stopped and turned to face him, looking up into his eyes with a direct challenge.

'And if I have? It's no concern of yours, is it?'

'It's a waste—and I dislike waste,' he said, his smile knowing, as if he had a long and intimate understanding of her requirements. 'You need a man who can light your fire—and you *do* have an inner fire, Cordelia, I know. Does he make you burst into flames when he touches you? If not, then you're settling for less than your due, and I think you know it.'

'This may be news to you, Gil,' she said curtly, 'but there are relationships between men and women that don't depend on...on...'

'Mutual attraction?' he suggested, a half-laughing gleam in his eyes.

'I was going to say, merely on sex,' she contradicted him haughtily.

'You don't know what you're talking about, my girl,' he told her. 'There's a whole spectrum of emotions a man and a woman can share, but without the chemistry there's a vital element missing.' He shook his head. 'Don't sell yourself short, Cordelia.'

The tension, the worry which had been mounting in her over these last, fraught days, finally came to a head, and her taut nerves reached snapping point.

'Oh, fine!' she exploded. 'The chemistry did a hell of a lot for Merche Ramirez and all the others, didn't it? I'm not panting for that experience, Gil. And how dare you try to tell me what I need? When I've got far more serious problems than whether or not to let some man into my bed! When I stand to lose my livelihood, possibly the roof over my head, and...oh, go away!'

She broke into a run, stumbled, almost falling into a flower bed, and he caught her easily, gripping both her shoulders in his strong hands and holding her captive. Two fugitive tears trickled down her cheeks, and her eyes were very dark and blue in her distraught face, her whole body suddenly as limp as a rag doll's.

Gil looked down at her, stern and tender at the same time, then drew her to a nearby wooden bench seat, one arm steady around her shoulders.

'Now tell me,' he said firmly, 'what *is* all this about?'

It was crazy and completely illogical. She had fought him, evaded him, tried to hate him, but now, with her defences down, and his arms holding her securely, it seemed the most natural thing in the world to unburden herself to him.

'The business is on the skids,' she said brokenly. 'I can't meet the repayments on the loan, especially now that the interest rates have gone sky-high. The bank can't advance me any more, and it seems the only way I can salvage anything is to sell. If I can even find a buyer right now, which won't be easy.'

'It's that bad?' he queried.

'It really is. And the irony is that, given a few months more, I feel sure I could turn the corner.' She sniffed miserably. 'There's nothing I can do.'

'I wouldn't say that.' His voice was curiously neutral, and she glanced up, quickly and suspiciously.

'If you're going to offer to lend me money, please don't, because I wouldn't accept,' she said swiftly.

'*Dios*, but you're prickly as a cactus!' he said wryly. 'Don't worry, I wasn't going to do any such thing. I don't want you to be beholden to me, and I don't want your gratitude.'

Even in her distress, she was capable of embarrassment at her misinterpretation of him.

'I'm sorry,' she mumbled, red-faced. 'I just thought...'

'You think wrongly, where I'm concerned, very frequently, but you don't learn. You go right on making the same mistake,' Gil said curtly. 'However——' his voice softened slightly '—to get back to your problem—there is a way you could make a large enough sum of money to more than tide you over, fairly quickly.'

Cordelia stared at him, puzzled. 'I don't understand.'

'You will, if you listen and stop interrupting,' he reprimanded, and she bit her lip, seized by an uncomfortable feeling that he was somehow enjoying this. 'Those sketches of yours, the ones you did in La Vega. If you let me use them to illustrate my book, you would then become my collaborator, and the publishers would make you a sizeable advance. Now.'

Everything around them had gone deathly quiet—or so it seemed to Cordelia. She could no longer hear the birds singing, the woods clicking on the bowling green, the distant shouts of children playing. Gil was offering her a way out. So why did she feel this strange sense of inevitability, as of one walking into a trap that had always been there, waiting...?

'You haven't found an illustrator yet?' she asked faintly.

'I haven't found anything nearly so good,' he said. 'I want those sketches, Cordelia. I've always wanted them. Let me have them, I'll take them to the publishers, and we'll get the deal set up. Then you'll have your money—up front, on the strength of what you've already done. I'll see they don't keep you waiting for a settlement until you submit the rest.'

'What do you mean—the rest?' she asked slowly, with foreboding growing in her. For she knew already—oh, yes, she knew! She would walk into his set trap with her eyes wide open, because she had no choice, could think of no other way of raising so much money, so quickly!

Gil Montero had been waiting for her, drawing her patiently and inexorably to him with the silent, implacable intentness of a grand master of chess. And now he had her, check and mate! It was with no surprise at all that she heard him say softly, 'But, Cordelia, you knew all along that they wouldn't be sufficient in themselves—that I needed more. Time to get out your pencils and paints, *cariña*. Time to go back to Spain, and finish what you started.'

CHAPTER NINE

SHE did, of course, have a choice. She was not under a duress so great that she *had* to do as he wished, regardless, or so she told herself.

But what a choice! She could sell the shop—and do what? After several years of being her own boss, independence had become an ingrained habit, and she thought she would make a very bad employee, even if anyone would employ her.

There were always loan sharks who would lend her the money at interest rates even more exorbitant than those she was already paying, but that would be robbing Peter to pay Paul, and she would surely end up more deeply in debt than ever. She would be foolish to turn down legitimate work which would solve her present financial problems, to embark upon such a course.

And yet... to go to Spain with Gil...? Was that not even greater foolhardiness? For he had made it clear that they would go together.

'The written part of the book is all but finished. I just have a few things to check out,' he had said. 'Besides, I have to go back. There are... other matters to attend to. Reasons why I must be there.'

His closed expression forbade discussion of those other matters, but Cordelia knew intuitively that Gil had not yet resolved the dilemma within him, that he was still working out his dual identity. Spain was calling him, quietly but insistently, and he had to answer.

Given that, and given, also, the fierce undercurrents of sensuality that had always bubbled and seethed below

the surface of their volatile relationship, she could fore-
see a sojourn fraught with endless complications. Each
of them had personal demons to exorcise, and on top
of that she had to contend with the violent attraction
which drew her to him. She had to know what his intentions were, and on what basis he expected them to
travel together.

'If I do go...' she had said slowly, and very cautiously
'...it would be a business trip purely, I gather? We would
be...simply colleagues? Am I right?'

She had picked her words very carefully and selec-
tively, avoiding any emotional or sexual connotations.
All the same, Gil's eyes were lowered suggestively, and
he favoured her with a long, slow, seductive smile.

'Why, Cordelia,' he said softly, 'I think you'll have
to answer that question for yourself. If you're asking
what I *think* you're asking...' he paused, his eyes holding
hers, dark and hypnotic '...I can only repeat that I've
never made love to any woman who hasn't wanted me
to.'

At that she had turned away, unable to bear the look
in his eyes. A warning voice inside her was telling her
clearly that she would find it hard...perhaps impossible...to go away with him and not give in to the
ever-increasing pressure of her own desire.

I always get what I want in the end, he had once told
her. He wanted her drawings for his book, and he wanted
her. Would this be the point, at last, where her surrender
would be inevitable?

Cordelia made one final bid to evade the net closing
skilfully around her.

'What about the shop?' she protested. 'Even if I had
the money from the publishers, it doesn't seem a good
idea to close it for an indefinite period now.'

'I've thought about that,' he said. 'There's no
problem, and you wouldn't need to close. Gaynor will

look after it for you. She's itching for something to do from now until she starts college, now that she's renounced a life of aimlessness. I know she enjoyed working here, and she'd make a good job of it.'

He had it all worked out so neatly that Cordelia found it hard to credit that he had planned it in the short time since he had learned of her difficulties. It was almost as if he had always intended that she should go back to Spain with him, and she wondered, with a shudder, what other means he would have found of coercing or persuading her, had not this opportunity conveniently cropped up.

He stood up, drawing her to her feet.

'Let's go,' he said forcefully. 'There are travel arrangements to be put in hand, and I must phone my publishers and tell them that the illustrator I want is finally... available.'

'I haven't agreed to any of this yet,' Cordelia said quickly, aware of a sensation of panic.

'I think you have,' Gil said calmly.

And the awful thing was that, while part of her resented and kicked against this high-handed taking over of her life, another part, deeper and not freely acknowledged, was exhilarated by it. She was riding a wave over which she had little or no control... but she had chosen to ride it. Was she free or a prisoner? Cordelia no longer knew.

Alone in her flat, she took out the sketches which had lain there, deliberately ignored, for so many months, and assessed them with a cool, critical eye. She knew they were good. The scenes jumped fresh and exciting from the page, the birds and flowers almost alive. Her dormant senses quivered, and her fingers ached, physically, for the feel of the pencils and brushes. She would do some watercolours, as well as the line drawings... even at this distance, she pictured in her mind the mountains around La Vega, planning what she would do.

She would be working—really working, creatively, at last, and who knew what that might release in her professionally? A sudden burst of energy crackled through the inertia which had held her like the Sleeping Princess through the last weeks. Spring raced through her veins. She was going to Spain with Gillan de Mornington... or with Gil Montero? Either, or both, he was the man she loved, and she would take whatever risks this journey involved.

From that moment things began to move very quickly. Gaynor arrived, keen to spend some time working with Cordelia, so that she knew more about the art side of the business before she had to handle it alone. She was bursting with enthusiasm, more alive and vivacious than Cordelia had ever seen her.

'I'm going *away* to college in September, had you heard?' she bubbled. 'Not that I don't love Mummy and Ran, and Gil has been absolutely superb—it's all down to him that I found the nerve to consider it at all! But I'll be a real student, with my own digs, and my own friends, and I'll be learning something useful. And I won't always have Alyssa looking down her exquisite nose at me at every end and turn!'

Cordelia laughed.

'You'll have a wonderful time, and you'll be an excellent student, I'm sure,' she said. 'Your family will miss you, but I'm sure they realise it's in your own best interest. How are they, by the way?'

Gaynor frowned.

'Well enough,' she said hesitantly. 'I think Mummy's coming round a bit—she's starting to go out more, and to entertain quite often.' She took a long, thoughtful breath. 'To tell you the truth, I think she could accept

Daddy's death more easily if there weren't this awful mystery in the background all the time.'

Something tingled along Cordelia's spine, telling her that here she was treading on quicksand, and that she would be wise to avoid this subject, if at all possible.

'Gaynor, I don't think you should discuss it with me,' she began. 'I'm not a member of the family, and...well, I just don't think you should.'

The other girl shook her head.

'Don't stop me, please, Cordelia,' she begged. 'I have to talk to someone, and you understand the situation. The thing is...it just doesn't add up. This man who, according to Gil, callously abandoned a woman and her child...who then remarried, and kept the whole thing a secret, for the rest of his life...'

She prowled the gallery, restlessly.

'This man was my father, my wonderful father, who gave Ran and me all we asked for...this was the husband my mother loved, and lived with all those years. He *wasn't* an unfeeling seducer, or a brute. I *know* this, because I knew him, and lived under the same roof with him. I've said so to Gil, but his experience is different, and he's not a liar, he's perfectly sincere in what he believes. It's like a kaleidoscope that you shake, and every time you get a different pattern. What's the truth? That's what I want to know!'

'I don't have any answers, Gaynor,' Cordelia said soberly. 'For what it's worth, I think it troubles Gil too. I think he's searching for the missing piece, just as you are.'

'We've hunted through all Daddy's papers, but there's nothing that throws any light on the matter,' Gaynor said bleakly. 'I've got this awful feeling that we'll probably never know what happened with his first marriage, or if he ever meant to tell us about it at some time. I hate not knowing. It casts a cloud over everyone...except Alyssa, who I don't think gives a hoot. The only thing that's annoying her is that Gil won't take her to Spain with him. Boy, is she angry about that!'

Cordelia glanced sharply across the room at Gaynor.

'She has no need to be. This is a business trip, not a pleasure jaunt,' she said briskly. 'Both Gil and I will be working, and Alyssa would certainly be bored out of her mind in La Vega.'

'Alyssa doesn't really believe that business trip thing,' said Gaynor, her eyes twinkling. 'She thinks Gil is taking you away because he fancies a final fling before he settles down with her. So she told me—in strictest confidence, of course! Nothing has been said to any of us, at home, and I don't really believe it, but according to her they're all but engaged.'

This conversation left Cordelia very thoughtful on several counts. She tormented herself endlessly by wondering if it was indeed true that Gil and Alyssa had some sort of understanding, and were 'all but engaged'. He had said nothing to her either, but if that reassured Gaynor it did nothing of the kind for Cordelia. But she knew she could never bring herself to ask him. Hadn't she known all along that if it were not Alyssa, it would be someone like her, and part of her did not want this confirmed, if it were so.

A fresh wave of emotion caught her in its wash—fear, guilt, panic. She should not be going away with a man who might already have chosen his marriage partner, even if, Gil being Gil, his choice had not been influenced by love. For although she kept on referring to it as a business trip, she had not convinced herself on that score, and her suspicions were not all that far from Alyssa's!

Right on cue, as if he were listening in to her unspoken doubts, Gil phoned.

'We're booked on a flight to Bilbao on Monday,' he told her. 'The publishers' advance will be paid into your bank account the same day.'

Cordelia laughed, without mirth.

'What uncanny timing! Is that to ensure that I don't snatch the money and back out of the deal?'

'You can't back out. You signed the contract,' he pointed out levelly. 'Besides, you're a businesswoman, Cordelia, and you wouldn't do that. There's only one area in which you tend to advance and then sound the retreat.'

Cordelia's face was as hot as a furnace, and she was about to slam down the phone when he said, deadly calm and quiet, but with utter authority, 'I wouldn't do that if I were you. I have a thousand and one things to organise before we leave, and I haven't time to waste making unnecessary phone calls. Now listen. We've to drive to the airport, so I'll pick you up at six-thirty precisely. Be ready.'

'I'll be ready,' she said tautly, trembling with rage, hating him again for having the power to call the shots, and wishing she did not love him so intensely at the same time.

It was true—she had signed the contract. She could not withdraw now, without losing the money, whatever professional credibility she could claim, and her own self-respect into the bargain. She was truly committed.

The plane touched down at Bilbao airport, and very quickly they were driving out in the waiting hire car along a velvet-smooth *autopista*.

Bilbao was a vast industrial port and city, but they were soon clear of it, and cruising through the pleasant Basque countryside, full of prosperous-looking farms with distant mountain views beyond.

Gil, as she knew all too well, could be a charming and entertaining companion when he chose, but neither on the journey to the airport, nor during the flight, had he so chosen. Instead, she had seen the other side of him, equally familiar to her, silent, aloof and withdrawn.

He was not, and never would be, an easy man to know or to understand in all his complexity, she reflected, but, knowing something of the conflicting forces tugging at him, she had kept mostly quiet herself, apart from necessary communication, or the odd casual comment.

Now she felt him tense, palpably, as Spain reclaimed him...and then relax. She waited for the chameleon-change of his personality, his very appearance, but it did not happen, and then she knew he would never again be the man she had first met last summer in La Vega. Mornington Hall had seeped into his very soul, and become a part of him. The Spanish he had spoken from childhood still came as easily and fluently as ever, when they stopped for petrol or food, but he was different, and he knew it too.

'They do say one can't go back,' he said, easing himself behind the wheel and putting the car in gear again. 'Most of the time, it isn't the places that change, but oneself. Life is a forward-moving process.'

This was the most revealing, the most personal remark he had permitted himself during the entire journey, so far, and Cordelia caught her breath slightly as she weighed her response.

'Is that a cause for regret?' she asked.

He smiled soberly.

'I'm not sure. It's simply a fact,' he said. 'I don't think I can be Gil Montero again.'

'Maybe you never really were,' she suggested, and he laughed a little sarcastically.

'How profound she is!' he declared, and Cordelia tightened her lips and stared straight ahead. He could hurt her so easily now, but she was determined not to let him know it.

Travelling through Spain with Gil at the wheel was an entirely different experience from driving with Bryce. He drove swiftly and confidently, intent on reaching their destination without delay. The roads gave him no reason for alarm, even when they left the coast and began to traverse the switchback defiles and passes of the Picos area. These were still his mountains, he was not afraid of them, and, strangely, Cordelia found she suffered none of the claustrophobic nervousness her earlier visit had induced.

The grey peaks still soared high into the pale blue sky, snow lingering on their heights; the road still snaked narrowly between them. But Gil was at her side, and she had the oddest sensation of being under a protective spell. As if, because she was with him, the mountains welcomed and sheltered instead of imprisoning her, and they would not harm or threaten her in his presence.

But while she could at last appreciate the stunning beauty and grandeur of this remote corner of Europe, as they drew nearer to their destination a different kind of tension began to build up in her. Gil had said nothing of what arrangements he had made for her in La Vega, and she had not liked to ask. He had a nice line in insinuating replies to such queries, which always left her flustered and nervous. She assumed she would be boarding at the *fonda* where she had stayed before…but with Gil nothing could *ever* be safely assumed, or taken for granted.

She drew in her breath as, rounding a bend, they came sharply into La Vega. The intervening months seemed to slip away, and she felt as if she had never left, it was all so oddly familiar. The one main street running through the village, with the *fonda*, and Antonio's shop where she had bought her walking shoes. The little lanes along which the cows trod, bells tinkling around their necks, the quaint *'horreos'*, little buildings on stilts, where the grain was stored. To her utter amazement, Cordelia felt a rush of what could only be described as affection for this remote rural scene. Yet when she had visited it before she had been conscious of fear, and a sense of alienation, within herself.

'It isn't the places that change—it's oneself,' Gil had said. Had *she*, then, changed so much in those months? Loving the man, had she grown, without realising it, to care for this place which had been so important to him?

She could hardly wait to see Gil's picturesque little house, but to her surprise he kept on driving.

'Why aren't we stopping?' she demanded, puzzled.

'It's getting late, and we should get involved in greeting the entire populace,' he said. 'You can't hurry these things in Spain. Everyone would want to buy us drinks, and one thing would lead to another. Best to come back another day, with time to spare.'

She frowned. 'Come back another day? I don't get it. Aren't we staying here? I mean, I assumed...'

Gil smiled faintly, with a touch of reproof.

'You do a lot of assuming, don't you? If you'd asked, I would have told you. We aren't staying in La Vega. I let my house there to a young couple who got married and needed somewhere to live. Who do you think is looking after the chickens and the cats?'

'And Pelayo?' she supplied.

'No, Pelayo's back with Luis, from whom I acquired him as a puppy. I miss him, but aside from the quarantine regulations, and the uncertainty of my own future when I left here, Pelayo's a mountain-bred dog. He'd be unhappy away from here.'

Cordelia suffered a pang of regret and surprise as it occurred to her that there were whole areas of Gil's life about which she knew little. She had been so deeply enmeshed in the sheer physical and emotional effect he had on her that she had never delved into these hidden recesses. It had to be said, too, that he did not always welcome or encourage such enquiries. She stole a glance at him now, as he drove, wishing she could know him better, but aware that a good measure of his attraction was that innate reserve—the little bit he always held back.

'Don't be too anxious,' he said. 'I'm not expecting you to camp by the roadside.'

'I'm not anxious,' she insisted quickly, 'merely curious. Where *are* we going?'

'Ah, now you'll have to wait and see,' he replied mysteriously.

They were well beyond the village now, the road climbing steeply and tortuously, inducing fearful hypertension, each dip and bend preceding a further ascent. In this high and lonely world, they passed an occasional tiny hamlet, now and then a car passed them going in the opposite direction, but for the most part they were alone.

'Up there,' said Gil, pointing to the misty peaks rising yet higher above them, 'is Covadonga, where the battle was fought which turned the tide of the Moorish invasion of Spain.'

'It's difficult to see how anyone could live and fight in such a fastness,' she said incredulously.

'But easy to understand how a small band of men who knew these mountains could hold them against all comers,' he said. 'There's a good road to Covadonga now, a vast church has been built there, and of course, it rakes in the tourists! Nevertheless, it helps one to understand the dour independence of the Asturian character. We aren't Latin, Mediterranean folk hereabouts.'

'*We?*' Cordelia queried softly, and he glanced swiftly at her before giving his attention back to the road.

'Freudian slip,' he murmured. 'You're too sharp by half, Miss Harris!'

The route broadened and dropped down to a more gentle, undulating valley as they approached the small town of Cangas de Onis. Cordelia registered quick, pleasing impressions of shops and cafés, a tree-shaded square where pigeons quested for crumbs and children rode bikes, a mediaeval bridge with a huge cross suspended from the central point of its arch, beneath which a silver river flowed. Mountains framed the town in whichever direction she looked, like a magnificent setting for a gem.

A short way beyond the town, Gil turned the car through what had once been a gateway, although now no gates hung there, and up a drive bordered by a neglected, deeply overgrown garden which still bore traces of loveliness, like a faded dowager. At the top of the drive stood a house touched with the same fading graciousness, a large, two-storeyed stone mansion with stucco peeling from its walls. Cordelia thought it had an air of having been unlived in for a long time, but as Gil stopped the car outside, the large front door opened and a middle-aged couple emerged.

Cordelia said, 'Gil? What's going on? Whose is this house, and who are these people?'

'Patience,' he counselled her soberly. 'The house, for your information, is now mine, and the couple, whom I haven't actually met before, are caretakers I engaged to look after it. All this has been of necessity arranged from a distance, but the place should be fit to live in. Or at least, it had better be!'

Cordelia watched from the car as he got out and talked to the caretakers. Her puzzlement was increasing by the minute. Why on earth had Gil bought this decaying mansion in its overgrown grounds, and was he, as it appeared, expecting them to stay here? That must be so, as the man was already lifting their luggage from the car and carrying it indoors, followed by his smiling wife.

Gil opened the car door and held out a hand to Cordelia. Like a sleepwalker she put hers into it, allowing him to draw her to her feet and lead her into the house. The warmth of his fingers had a hypnotic effect on her, and she felt she was being drawn into some kind of enchanted palace, just stirring from a long sleep. The wooden floors had been polished to a high golden shine, and from the hall he ushered her into a spacious *sala*, furnished with vast, comfortable chairs and dark oak occasional tables. A fire burned in an enormous hearth, against the impending chill of the spring evening, and before it, on an Afghan carpet of some age but undeniable quality, a black and white cat slept serenely.

Cordelia at last awoke from her trance, and turned towards Gil, half smiling.

'Do you ever live anywhere that doesn't have animals in residence?' she asked.

'No, and I trust I never shall.' Still holding her hand, he drew her to a sofa in front of the fire. 'Sit down, Cordelia. There is, as I recall, a dining-room, but for tonight, the caretaker's wife, whose name is Blanca, will bring us something to eat in here.'

She glanced out of the windows at the profuse entanglement of shrub and weeds in the garden, and then back at him.

'As you recall? You know this house? You've lived here before?' she guessed, still deeply puzzled by their arrival here, and the strangeness of the entire situation.

'Yes. And it gives me deep satisfaction to have it back where it belongs—in my ownership,' he told her. 'This is the house where my mother was born, and where I lived when she brought me back to Spain as a small child. After she died, I lived here with an elderly aunt, but...' he paused, frowning painfully '...we fell on hard times, and had to let it go.'

He had released her hand, and she missed the warmth of the contact with his. Twisting slightly towards him in her seat, she said, 'I remember now, you told me your mother came from Cangas de Onis. But what did you do then, after you had to leave here?'

She hoped he would not fall into one of his sudden uncommunicative moods, at this moment. It was suddenly crucial to her that she filled in these gaps in his life story, to help her stumble towards a fuller understanding of the whole man.

'We lived in a small, rented house in Cangas de Onis, and every day I had to walk past here and see other people living in it,' said Gil, with a hint of bitterness. 'Then they left, and it's stood empty for many years. Not that it made any difference to me. I was never in a position, until now, to afford to buy it, or to restore it. After my aunt died, I was farmed out among a series of ageing relatives, and by the time I reached college age I was alone.'

He reached out and gently tickled the stomach of the black and white cat, which stretched sensuously and began to purr. His face was in shadow, but Cordelia did not need to see it to pick up his remembered feelings of loss and loneliness. They were clarion-clear in his quiet voice.

'But you came to England—to university?' she prompted.

'Yes, with the help of a scholarship and what little money my mother had left me,' he said. 'I read English and Hispanic Studies. In the holidays I crammed English kids for O-Level Spanish, or I came back here and...'

'Crammed Spanish kids for the English equivalent,' she supplied. 'It can't have been easy. But, Gil, you come from a wealthy family. Did it never occur to you to look up your father?'

'No,' he said curtly, 'it did not. He knew where to find me, if he so wished.'

Her heart twisted with sudden pity for the young student working his way to a degree, too proud to ask for the help to which his birth entitled him. She began to understand why he had been, for so long, like a cat that stalked alone, trusting no one too far, allowing himself to care for no one too deeply, haunted always by the spectre of betrayal and rejection. And that, presumably, was why he had then turned his back on the English side of his heritage and returned to Asturias to live.

'So you finally came back here, when you were through studying?' she said, compelled to trace the route which had led him to Merche Ramirez, and thence to La Vega. 'What did you do then?'

His face hardened and closed suddenly, as if he feared that by telling her so much, he had opened up a breach in his own fierce defences.

'Many things,' he said, deliberately vague. 'Some of them not fit for your ears, others too boring to mention. Ah, here comes supper.'

Blanca was still smiling, almost permanently, as she bustled in with a tray, and a delicious aroma accompanied her. She had prepared a traditional Asturian dish of *fabes con almeja*, white beans and fried clams in a kind of stew, with it there was bread, a carafe of robust red wine, and a large wedge of strong Cabrales cheese.

'Good peasant food,' said Lord de Mornington appreciatively, as he tucked in without hesitation. 'Come on, Cordelia—eat. Tomorrow we must both start work.'

There was an unreal quality to all this for Cordelia. Sitting with Gil in this room which he had known as a child, eating supper and watching the spring dusk closing in outside, the flames leaping in the grate, the caretaker's cat yawning and purring at their feet. England, and the life she had lived there, seemed a world away; tomorrow, as he had reminded her, she must embark on the work she had promised to do. Tonight there was only herself and Gil, set down in this house as if on a stage, apart from everything and everyone.

Blanca came in, drew the blinds, lit the lamps, and brought a pot of fresh coffee.

'*Muchas gracias,*' said Cordelia, in her still halting Spanish. '*Ha sido una comida excelente!*'

She smirked triumphantly at Gil, and he pulled a wry face. 'Nice try—but we must do something about your accent!' he teased.

Blanca picked up the tray to remove it.

'*Señora,*' she beamed at Cordelia.

'No, *señorita,*' Gil corrected her. 'Señorita Harris.'

Cordelia looked down, and kept her eyes from meeting Gil's until Blanca had left the room. She knew her transparent redhead's skin was flushed deeply in the firelight, not because of the flames, but because the caretaker's wife had addressed her as '*señora*'. What relationship had she presumed Cordelia enjoyed with Gil? Did she think she was Lady de Mornington? What, if anything, had he told her? He had just corrected her very promptly, making it quite clear that Cordelia was 'Miss Harris'.

'Don't worry, Cordelia,' he said softly, with that uncanny ability to tune in to her thoughts. 'This is not La Vega. You will not be considered a ruined woman because you are sleeping under the same roof as I am.'

She could not answer, but her heart had begun to race, and there was a strange singing in her ears. She forced herself to pour the coffee without spilling it, to keep her hand steady as she lifted the cup to her lips. But all the time his eyes were on her, and she was aware of the strangest feeling. As if, in his mind, he was already making love to her, and without his having touched her at all, she could feel her own response leaping to meet him, starting deep down, in the pit of her stomach, and spreading out through her body with fingers of delicious, tingling warmth.

He finished his coffee and waited, silent and still watchful, as she finished hers. Then he uncoiled swiftly, stood up, and said, 'Come with me.'

Without hesitation, Cordelia rose and walked at his side out into the hall. In England, she might have resisted, might have fought this easy assumption of her surrender with anger and resentment, with a protest against being so used. But this was Spain, and a different Cordelia had begun to emerge, who saw the bolts and springs of fate at work, and acknowledged that only fear had kept her, for so long, from this destiny.

Side by side they climbed the broad flight of still uncarpeted stairs to the first floor. Gil did not touch her—deliberately, she thought, arousing and playing on her growing desire to be touched. Along a corridor—still with several inches of carefully maintained space between them—past several closed doors, she sensed him finding his way by memory—until he stopped outside the one he was seeking.

He smiled gravely down at her.

'I hope this is how I planned it,' he said suddenly, unexpectedly.

'Doubts, Gil?' she queried, with a little laugh, anticipation all but snapping her tautly strung nerves, waiting for the moment when he took her in his arms, and at last she stopped fighting him. 'How unlike you!'

His hand touched her arm as he pushed open the door—whether by accident or by design she wasn't sure, but her bare skin tingled with a pleasure so intense it frightened her. It was dim and shadowy on the landing, and his face was only a dark outline looming above her. She sighed, swayed slightly towards him, and then he switched on the bright overhead lights in the room, and she gasped out loud.

She had expected a bedroom, but this was a studio! A large, airy studio with big windows which would let in the maximum of light, and polished wood flooring. There was a large table, a desk, and over by the window, an easel. Stacks of canvases, tubes of oil paint, palettes and knives, watercolours. Endless paper, pencils and chalks, bottles of white spirit. An easy chair for moments of repose, a coffee-making machine. The complete artists' hideaway.

Cordelia turned to him, speechless, eyes wide blue lakes of incomprehension, and he smiled back, enjoying her incredulity.

'Is there everything you need?'

She took a few halting steps into the room, gazing around her.

'Everything...' She shook her head, as if to clear it. 'Gil, all this stuff is from my own shop, in Hereford!'

'Naturally. It's a good order, why place it elsewhere?' he said practically. 'I got Gaynor to organise it. It wasn't difficult; I just used a false name for the invoice.'

Reaction had begun to set in. She had accompanied him upstairs, every nerve-end alive with apprehensive desire, expecting him to make love to her, and so incredibly willing...no, eager...that she was half ashamed of herself. And she had been so sure that was what Gil had planned, and why he had brought her here in the first place.

She had miscalculated hopelessly, proving yet again that she did not really know him at all. Hating herself, she lashed out at him in her frustration.

'You like playing this sort of trick on me, don't you?' she accused him. 'It seems to amuse you! This is all very grand, but I don't need it! I don't need half of this equipment to do a few sketches. Everything I want I've brought with me!'

'True,' he said imperturbably. 'But you might need it in order to produce real art, for your first exhibition.'

Angry tears sprang to her eyes, and she clenched her fists tightly.

'You can't do this, Gil! It doesn't work that way!' she declared furiously. 'You can't shut me in a room and order me to paint, just like that! I can't "produce art", as you put it, to order!'

'Get a hold on yourself, Cordelia,' he said brusquely. 'No one is going to shut you in, and you're under no obligation other than that in the publishers' contract. I told you, I don't require your gratitude. However, a little appreciation might not have been misplaced.'

Gil shrugged.

'Maybe one day you will grow up sufficiently to stop suspecting me of having ulterior motives for everything I do. Let me know when that happens.'

Turning abruptly, he strode along the landing. Pausing at the top of the stairs, he looked briefly over his shoulder at her. 'Blanca tells me your bedroom is next door to the studio. I'm going to look round the garden before it's completely dark, so I'll wish you goodnight.'

He was gone, then, leaving her standing there alone, feeling small and shaken, and utterly in the wrong.

CHAPTER TEN

CORDELIA lay sleepless for a long time, in a vast *cama matrimonial* in the room next to the newly appointed studio. She heard vague sounds from downstairs, Blanca and her husband, Tomás, moving around in their quarters. She heard, also, Gil's unmistakable footsteps as he came in from the garden and went to his own room. He did not pause outside her door.

Exhausted, she finally slept, and did not wake until Blanca brought her a tray with a pot of coffee, and opened the shutters to a bright morning.

Beyond her window, the neglected garden sparkled with early dew. There were tangled old rose bushes, wildly proliferating flowering shrubs, well enough established to survive despite being choked with weeds. Paths sprouting grass from between the paving stones, cracked urns and statuary, a small pond thickly covered in green algae. On a moss-covered sundial, the black and white cat sunned himself, nonchalantly licking his paws, and in the distance the Picos were crisp and clear, thrusting their still white heads into a cloudless sky.

Cordelia dressed quickly and nervously in a green and white print cotton voile dress and white sandals, forcing her thick mass of curls into an emerald-green clasp at the nape of her neck. Apprehension gripped her fiercely—she was afraid of meeting Gil this morning, although she knew it was a hurdle that had to be surmounted.

Last night they had been deeply at cross purposes. She had expected a planned and prearranged seduction, like a scene from a bad movie, she thought disgustedly. Convincing herself that she was a victim of fate, and that she had no say in the matter, she had allowed herself to believe that the whole thing was out of her hands.

She should have known well enough that that was not Gil's style. He wanted her not only willing, but consciously choosing this path, of her own volition. 'You will come to me one day of your own free will... I wouldn't make love to you unless you invited me to...' He wanted her to admit defeat, to beg him to take her. He wanted nothing less than her voluntary and unconditional surrender.

Irresistibly, she found herself opening the door to the studio, walking around, fingering the virgin canvases, touching the fine sable brushes. Everything here was of the highest quality, no expense spared, the kind of equipment she scraped and saved to obtain for herself. Cordelia frowned and bit her lip. Why had Gil gone to all this trouble on her account, if he was not expecting payment in full? She did not understand him. He was still an enigma to her, and always would be, although she loved him not one iota less for that.

The Montero house was larger than she had appreciated at first glance, last night. Tiptoeing downstairs and along echoing wood-panelled corridors, she realised that Gil's mother, although not in the same league as the de Morningtons, must have come from an old and respected family, who had somehow lost their money. It would appear that Gil was the sole survivor of their line, and that he stood there, at the very apex of two proud old traditions, which he alone could forge into a cohesive whole. She swallowed painfully. No wonder there was no real place for her in his scheme, she told herself soberly.

Across the corridor from the lounge where they had eaten supper last night, a door stood open, and Cordelia saw that this was the dining-room Gil had mentioned. He was already there, seated at a long refectory-type table, a pot of coffee in front of him, leaning on one elbow, dark head bent over what looked like a pile of bills and estimates. A frown of utter concentration furrowed his brow, he was entirely unaware of her presence, and her heart turned over with a burst of pure love. Not simply the wrench of desire he always, and easily, aroused in her, but a fierce need to help, to give, to understand. To be a part of his life for as long as he needed her, and in whatever capacity.

'Hello.' She tapped shyly on the door to attract his attention. He looked up, half smiling, pushing lean fingers through his already tousled hair.

'Come in. Have some coffee.' He waved her vaguely to a seat. 'I was just looking through some of these estimates for work needed on the house. I haven't actually arranged for anything to be done yet, because I wanted to see the place before I put anything major in hand.'

Cordelia slipped into a chair, still a little nervous, overcome by the new immensity of loving emotion which had seized her.

'The garden certainly is in need of a lot of work,' she suggested.

'You're not wrong. And the house, as you can see, is only half furnished. The reason for that is that I wanted to keep what remained of the original stuff, and dispose of all the rubbish the last owners acquired. The paintwork needs re-doing, the exterior rendering is in a frightful state, and there's woodworm in some of the panelling——' he laughed. 'That's just for starters!'

'It will take forever, Gil.'

'It's a labour of love, Cordelia. I may or may not ever live here for any length of time, but it's something I have to do.'

Cordelia paused as Blanca brought them breakfast—
eggs, *tostadas*, fruit juice and more coffee—and then in
a low voice, she said, 'Gil, I'm sorry.'

He looked at her from beneath coolly raised eyebrows, and she went on in a rush, allowing herself no
time to back out.

'About the studio. You . . . you took me by surprise. I
simply hadn't expected it, but it was wrong of me to
throw it all in your face. Forgive me.'

'De nada,' he said levelly, and his complete lack of
emotion caused her to cry out in furious anguish.

'But it isn't nothing! You went to all that trouble and
expense for me, and I can't repay it . . . I can't . . .'

'Cordelia,' he said firmly, silencing her with a look
of gentle but determined authority, 'forget it. The money
I have, in abundance, and it isn't important. What are
we talking about, here—a few pots of paint and rolls of
canvas? All I did was sign the cheque, so don't go
overboard.'

Cordelia bit her lip and subsided, thoroughly
chastised.

'Now then,' he went on, in the same stern, school-
masterly, almost avuncular tone, 'you have some sketches
to do for my book, which shouldn't take you too long,
considering that you rattled off the last lot in one
morning.'

'That's the idea—they're sketches,' she said
defensively.

'Precisely. I want them to be good, and I know they
will be. But they're not going to consume your every
waking moment, and meanwhile the studio is there. *You*
are here. And all *this* is out there.' He flung out a hand
to embrace the garden, the sky, the mountains. 'Damn
it, Cordelia, if you can't paint here, you can't paint anywhere! Are you an artist, or are you just one of those

boring would-be's, who sit around lamenting their inability to get it together?'

She jumped to her feet so abruptly that the chair fell over behind her, and outrage quivered in every line of her delicate body, her red curls escaping from the barrette as she tossed her head.

'How dare you?' she gasped. 'What right do you have to insult me like this? I've painted all my life—I painted long before I ever met you, and I'll paint again! You'll see! What do *you* know about it, anyhow?'

A slow, triumphant grin spread across his face.

'Very little,' he admitted freely. 'I'm merely doing what my ancestors did before me—I'm being a patron of the arts. Why do you think I brought you here, Cordelia? Hm?' He paused, head on one side, regarding her challengingly, daring her to answer.

In that moment, her pride was at rock bottom, her life was in ashes, and she could sink no deeper into despair. Wrong, wrong, wrong, a voice was screaming in her head, you had it all wrong! Gil hadn't brought her here because he desired her... not more than casually, passingly, although even last night, she could have sworn that he did still want her, as, undoubtedly, he once had.

She had played the waiting game too long, holding out, wanting him but afraid to follow through, and he had tired of it... as she might have known all along that he would. He was too experienced, too world-weary, and too devastatingly attractive to any number of women to be amused for long by her tentative innocence.

She had fallen in love with him, knowing all too well the hopelessness of that, but now, it seemed, she had failed to keep alive the only thing she might have had... his desire for her. He was bored with that now, and his life was too full of other, more urgent concerns. His full and ever increasing involvement with the de Mornington estate, his business affairs and charity work... his preoccupation with restoring the Montero house, his soon-to-be-published book. And in time, no doubt, there would be marriage... possibly to Alyssa?

'Very well,' she said quietly, and with immense dignity, never knowing where it came from, this sudden excess of strength, pride and fortitude. 'If that's the way you want it—so be it!'

Turning, she stalked out of the room, back straight, head high, heart breaking—but silently, invisibly, unseen, like a deep, internal wound, or melting snow. Without looking back, she went upstairs, into the studio, and closed the door firmly behind her.

At some point early in the proceedings she slipped into her bedroom, stripped off the green and white dress, and put on jeans and a loose shirt. She was barely conscious of taking this action, it was more of an automatic reflex, making herself comfortable to work. After that, she did not emerge from the studio all day. Her face composed in concentration, lips taut, she set up the easel, stretched the canvas over it, and began furiously and intently mixing her paints.

She did not stop to think. Usually she worked from life, with the subject, or at the very least a sketch or a photograph, in front of her. Now she worked swiftly and steadily from pure memory, turning her inner, artist's eye on her thoughts, her love and longing pouring out of her in the only way she had left.

Behind her, in the distance, the Picos glittered in the sun, green and beautiful, but she had her back to them, and no landscape took shape on her canvas. Instead she saw Gil's face, coming alive beneath her brushes. The quizzical arch of his eyebrows, the faint, tender-cynical smile, the fathomless eyes. She captured him, and briefly he was hers. But not for long, even now, for in time she would give him back to the world.

She had no idea of how long she existed in this frenzy of released creative passion. Time no longer had any relevance, she was entirely alone and self-sufficient, aware of neither hunger, thirst, fatigue, nor any other need. All the empty months since she last held a brush dropped away, and she did not have to ask, or wonder what she should do. She simply did it.

Only when at last there was a soft but undeniably peremptory tap on the door did she pause, stretch, and realise that her shoulders were stiff, her wrists aching, and her throat dry.

The door opened, although she had not spoken or given anyone permission to enter, but it was Gil, and since when had anyone's consent stood between him and his intentions? He carried a small tray laden with fresh lemon juice, cheese and fruit, which he set down on the table.

Cordelia blinked; her eyes were like dark bruises in her pale face as she gazed at him.

'What time is it?' she asked, like a sleepwalker.

'Two-thirty.' He looked at her across the room, the air still, but vibrant with implications between them, as if they stood either side of a minefield.

Cordelia rubbed a paint-smeared hand across her cheek. 'You should have told me it was getting late,' she said, coming awkwardly out of her trance and back to painful reality.

'*Dios*, I did not dare disturb you!' he said with a wry smile. 'I thought I was merely poking the fire, not setting alight a volcano! Having lit the blue touch paper, I thought it seemed prudent to retire.'

'Very amusing!' Her answering smile was wary. 'You knew what you were doing—you always do. And now you're going to say, "It worked, didn't it?"'

'Well, you're painting, aren't you?' he challenged.

'Indeed,' she conceded. 'But how do you know if I'm worth the expense of bringing me to Spain and setting me up?' As the hurtful feeling began to flow back into her, she could not resist a final taunt. 'In short, milord, you don't know if you'll get any return on your investment.'

Gil had picked up the jug to pour out the juice, and she saw, as he set it down on the tray with a ringing crack, a sharp anger flash in his eyes; his body tensed swiftly, violently, and he was across the room in a couple of impatient, furious strides.

'*Dios*, this time you've tried me too far!' he hissed. His hand grasped her wrist so hard the paintbrush jerked from it and fell to the floor. She stared into his face, no longer afraid, dark eyes and blue locked in an equality of rage and misunderstanding.

And then, looking down, he saw what he had been unable to see from where he stood before, because now he had the canvas fully in front of him, and he was gazing, head-on, at his own face.

'My God!' he exclaimed. 'Is *this* what you've been doing all day?'

'It...it isn't finished,' Cordelia said shakily.

He looked from the portrait to her face, and slowly the anger faded from his eyes. Something new, an expression she had never seen in them before, took its place...a wondering, regretful tenderness, a tentative hope...as if he had seen something he might believe in, but still doubted its existence.

'You have paint on your face,' he said. Glancing around for a clean cloth, and not seeing one, he released her wrist and gently rubbed a finger across her smudged cheek. 'Hell, I'm only making it worse!'

'It doesn't matter,' she said faintly, dizzy now from the closeness of him, from the brush of his fingertips on her skin. She shivered, gazed up at him, seeing, with

a fresh surge of joy and triumph, the naked desire in his
eyes which she had thought never to see again. He cupped
both his hands around her face and looked intently down
into her eyes, and she knew it was here and now—the
one moment which would otherwise pass her by, perhaps
forever. Their paths converged at this very point, or they
did not meet at all.

'Please...' she said, her voice so low it was barely
audible. 'Please, Gil——'

His own laughter was soft.

'Please what? Pour you a drink? Get the hell out?
How am I supposed to know what it is you're asking
me? I suppose it will have to do,' he teased, but his mouth
was already covering her throat with kisses, his fingers
working deftly at the buttons of her shirt.

There was nothing in the way of comfort, only a dust
sheet she had spread over the floor to protect it from
paint splashes, but no power could have stopped him
now, and her own desire was so urgent she was beyond
shame, as he undressed her and shrugged swiftly out of
his clothes. Naked on the paint-smeared sheet, she allowed him to release, at last, the sensual woman he had
first discovered and aroused in La Vega, arching and
turning her body every way he desired of her, giving and
taking pleasure so intense that in its final moments a
deep oblivion overcame her, and briefly she left her conscious self behind.

She had a brief recollection of being lifted and carried
bodily from the room, but the next thing she knew, they
were safely ensconced in the *cama matrimonial* in her
bedroom, Gil's arms were around her, the strong length
of his body warmly entwined with hers.

'What...?' She looked up at him, almost shy again,
not believing that passionate, abandoned female had
been herself.

'You blacked out,' he told her, smiling. 'I'm very flattered. I've never made that happen to anyone before.'

She stirred, the blissful tide receding as she remembered all the others . . . Gil's women, of whom she was
now just one more.

'I wouldn't have thought it was a novel experience for
a man of the world such as yourself,' she said drily.

He half turned towards her, touching the tip of her
nose lightly with one finger.

'Cordelia, what is this notion you have about
my . . . er . . . sexual voracity, and where did you get it
from?' he asked amusedly.

'Oh, Gil, don't pretend!' she cried. 'I learned all about
you from Merche Ramirez, of course, and according to
her, there were many others.'

He was silent for a moment, then he sighed.

De acuerdo,' he said. 'Very well—there may have been
a time . . . no, I will be honest, there *was* a time when I
played the field fairly energetically. When I first came
back to live in Spain, I drifted a lot. Moved from place
to place, from job to job. I was . . . looking for something, I suppose, and, not finding it within myself, I
didn't have much respect for others. Women seemed to
like me, for some reason. It came easily, and I took advantage of it.'

He raised himself on one elbow and caught her hand,
imprisoning it against the warmth of his chest. 'I was
not a nice man to know, I dare say. Perhaps I still am
not.'

Cordelia opened her mouth to speak, but he shook
his head.

'No, let me finish. All I can say in mitigation is that
La Vega was a kind of salvation for me,' he explained.
'It gave me stability. Oh, don't mistake me, I'm no saint,
but I lived more austerely there. It's no place for a rake.
I found a measure of peace, learned to accept myself,

carved out a niche. That's why I was reluctant to leave it.'

'But you did,' she said. 'You came to Mornington Hall and found another niche, one that might have been tailor-made for you.'

He frowned faintly.

'You know very well it wasn't that easy. But the unexpected happened. I did feel at home there, as if it had been waiting for me, and I for it. And not only had I acquired a family, but I began to feel affection for them. Evelyn has been wonderful, considering I disinherited her own son, *and* I now have a brother and a sister.'

Cordelia moved in his arms, drawing away from him a little.

'And a cousin,' she could not help reminding him. 'Had you forgotten Alyssa?'

'A distant cousin,' he corrected her. 'Don't *you* become distant, *querida*. I want you right here.'

Cordelia did not have the heart to pursue the unpleasant subject of Alyssa. *She* was here, in Gil's arms, and whatever the future held, he was hers at this moment.

'So you aren't angry with me any more, for luring you to England?' she asked.

'Not if you aren't angry with me for luring you back to Spain.' He stirred restlessly. 'But I wish I knew what my father had intended—what was in his mind. Whether he'd meant at some stage to tell his family about me, or if he found my existence so distasteful he'd simply tried to forget about it.'

'Gil,' Cordelia closed her arms around him, 'you have to accept that you'll probably never know, so you have to let go of it. Does it really matter so much?'

'It matters,' he insisted fiercely. 'Either I'm in my rightful place at Mornington Hall, or in spite of being legally entitled I shall always feel I'm something of a usurper.'

Then he smiled.

'You talk too much, Cordelia, and you make *me* talk too much. I don't want to talk, right now. I've waited so long for you, I only want to make love to you, again——' he kissed her lips tantalisingly, '—and again——' his mouth traced more kisses along the line of her throat '—and again.'

Until you tire of me, she thought with sudden despair, but it was too late now to turn back the clock. Passion flared between them again, and she forgot everything but her love for him.

The hours fled. Time had no meaning, and the light had begun to fade from the sky when at last they made their way downstairs, showered, dressed, and holding hands like two naughty children.

'I wonder what Blanca thinks we've been doing all afternoon,' Cordelia giggled.

'Lord knows, but she's a model of tact,' Gil replied. 'I hope there's food—I'm ravenous.'

There was indeed food, this time served properly in the dining-room, an immense dish of rabbit stew which had probably been simmering in the oven for hours, aromatic with herbs. Fruit, the inevitable cheese, and a variety of gloriously sticky pastries with syrup. Wine, of course, and coffee, which they drank in the *sala*, sitting on the floor in front of the fire, with the cat purring between them.

Cordelia looked neither forward nor back. She lived resolutely in this perfect, present moment, refusing to anticipate future pain or sorrow. She went willingly into Gil's arms yet again, in a perfection of physical and emotional fulfilment she had never dreamed of, and slept at last, with her head on his shoulder.

But in the morning, when she awoke, he was not there, and such a cold sense of deprivation stole over her that she shivered in the brilliant spring sunshine. It had felt so right, when they made love, so complete, that she had allowed herself to forget that he was not really hers, and that she played no part in his future.

She shook herself, forcibly dispelling these dark thoughts. Today she would paint again, work on her portrait. She was once again an artist, and it was Gil who had given her back her faith in herself and her ability. She was also a woman in love, her senses and her emotions gloriously and painfully alive. Be glad for what you have, here and now, she told herself.

She found him in the dining-room, once again absorbed in a pile of papers which were spread all over the table. The coffee stood untouched in the pot in front of him, and although he sat as still as a rock, waves of energy emanated from him, filling the room with a vibrant, purposeful, jubilant force.

'Good morning,' she said tentatively. It seemed a formal greeting to a man in whose arms you had spent the night, and who had left you to wake alone, but she could think of nothing better to say, and she was halted in her tracks by the almost electrical waves of excitement that possessed him.

He looked up, and his eyes were blazing with power; he smiled, a smile so brilliant it all but stunned her.

'Cordelia!' he said, his voice hoarse with emotion. 'You're not going to believe this, but look——'

He leapt to his feet, seized her hand, and drew her towards the table, laughing triumphantly.

'What is it, Gil?' she asked, bemused.

'I woke very early,' he told her. 'You looked so peaceful, I didn't want to disturb you, so I started roaming about the house, exploring the attics where I used to play as a child.'

He eased her into a chair, pressing down on her shoulders with those hard, strong hands she loved so much.

'I've been barking up the wrong tree all the time, turning Mornington Hall upside down in search of any old scrap of paper that would tell me the truth about myself and my parents. But it's all here, Cordelia. The people who lived in the house must simply have left all the junk in the attic. There are letters my father wrote to my mother, after she came back to Spain. Letters she tried to write to him, but never posted——'

A sudden cloud darkened his face, and instinctively, Cordelia laid her hand over his.

'So much anguish caused by two people who started out loving each other,' he said. 'All these years, I saw it in black and white, but it wasn't so simple. My mother was bitter, Cordelia. She felt wronged. But——' he hesitated, and she saw that for him, too, this knowledge had come hard and painfully. Then he straightened, accepted the pain, absorbed it, and made himself go on. 'She wronged him too. And she never told me the whole truth.'

His fingers closed over hers, and he held tightly to her hand as he told her the story he had at last been able to piece together.

Giles de Mornington and Maria Rosario Montero had fallen in love and married, perhaps foolishly, very young, and in the teeth of his family's opposition. Maybe if the de Morningtons had accepted the fearful young Spanish bride, the story might have ended differently. But she was lonely and unhappy in her enforced exile, homesick for her mountains, her own people, and her own language.

'She never learned to speak English very well,' Gil said. 'She thought that England was a cold, unfriendly place, full of unloving people, and she told me that my father cast her aside and sent her away. But see—it wasn't like that, as these letters plainly show. She wanted to go home, she cried and begged to go home. In the end, he

rather foolishly made her choose, and she chose Spain.
She bolted for home, taking me with her. That had *not*
been agreed. She just upped and took me.'

'The de Mornington heir,' Cordelia said slowly. 'He
could have fought her through the courts for custody.'

'He could,' Gil agreed, 'but he didn't. There's a whole
pile of correspondence in which he asks for my return,
to be educated here, to spend time in England. He appeared to have realised, a little late, that he must put his
foot down with his family and fight for his son's place.
But she clung on, and wouldn't let me go. It becomes
acrimonious——' He rifled through the dusty papers and
set a page in front of Cordelia. 'Here he is, refusing to
support or acknowledge me unless she agrees to send me
to England. She called his bluff and refused—but he
wasn't bluffing.'

Gil ran his free hand through his hair, and managed
a wry grin. '"Heav'n has no rage, like love to hatred
turn'd"?' he quoted ruefully.

Cordelia could scarcely breathe, so suffocatingly fierce
was the emotion holding them bound together at that
moment.

'So that's how it was,' he said. He spoke lightly, but
she knew, now, that this was when he felt most strongly.
'For a long time there was silence. Then, after she died,
he met and married Evelyn, and there's one more
letter...a letter he wrote to me, which I never received.'

He sighed. 'Perhaps I'd left Cangas by then, and the
new people here didn't know where to find me. Perhaps
they were just careless, and the letter was tossed up here,
with all the other stuff.'

'Your father wrote to *you*?' she asked breathlessly.

'In person. The only communication we shall ever
have.' Gil's voice was tight with controlled feeling. 'He
told me his side of the story...biased his way, of course,
but no more so than my mother's account. He was no
more a saint than I am! He also told me that he'd met

and married a wonderful woman, that he dared not tell her the sordid story of his first marriage, for fear of losing her love and respect, but that one day, when he was more sure of her, he would.'

'He put it off for a long time,' Cordelia said wryly.

'Which goes to prove that we must live every day as if there are no second chances,' Gil said feelingly. 'But he also wrote that in spite of everything I was still his heir, and asked me if I might wish to reply to his letter. He suggested, very tentatively, that it might not be too late for him to be my father.'

'Oh, Gil!' cried Cordelia, wrung by the pathos of it. 'If only that letter had reached you! You thought he'd rejected you... and then he must have thought you'd rejected *him*! What a sad, awful story!'

'I know,' he said. 'It's a chapter of errors on all sides. But at least I can tell Evelyn and Ran, and poor Gaynor, the truth. Her husband, their father, wasn't a monster. Just a misguided man with strong passions, who made mistakes.'

He stood up, disentangling himself from her hand, and walked over to the window.

'And now, finally, I know who I am,' he said. 'I know I hold Mornington not just because of some legal default, but because my father wished me to.'

He had his back to her, but she heard the pride, the vindication, and yes, the joy, ringing in his voice. The bitterness was gone, and so too was the rift that had divided him into two separate and warring entities. The two had now fused coherently into one—he was Gillan de Mornington Montero, and his place was wherever he wanted it to be. Here, in Spain, whenever he chose, and at Mornington Hall, with a suitably well-connected wife at his side.

Certainly he did not now need *her*, and Cordelia thought it best if she bowed out at once, while she could

still do so with dignity, and without betraying how much
it was hurting her.

'I'm glad for you, Gil,' she said quietly. 'Truly I am.
And I'm grateful to you too, because...because you
made me an artist again. And you taught me how to be
a woman. I'll always remember that.'

He turned round slowly.

'Remember it?' he repeated, his face darkening. '*Dios*,
do you think I'm likely to let you forget?'

She backed away as he crossed the room towards her.

'No, Gil, please... What happened between us
was...well, it happened, but I think it's best if we end
it now...'

'Oh, do you, indeed?' he demanded. His hands seized
her shoulders roughly, giving her an angry little shake.
'And what game were we playing yesterday, huh? What
were you doing in bed with me, acting as if I was the
only man in the world who meant anything to you? Was
that all it was—acting? Don't you know that I love
you...that I refuse to let you go?'

He shook her again, as if he would kill her, then folded
her close in his arms, as though he would refuse to let
anything harm her. But Cordelia was deaf to his contra-
diction. She had only heard three words that mattered,
three words she had never imagined she would hear him
say.

'You said you loved me!' she gasped. 'Gil, don't make
me suffer, if it's not true! I can't bear it. I love *you* too
much for that!'

'Of course it's true!' he groaned agonisedly. 'I never
knew it until I saw you out with that fellow Bryce, and
realised I couldn't bear the idea of you with another man.
Before that, I never loved a woman...I didn't know I
was capable of it! Why do you think I went to the trouble
of setting up the studio for you, bringing you out here?
I wanted you to realise your potential, but more than

that, I was afraid you'd never love *me* until you'd found your own way once more.'

'But I've loved you for so long,' she said incredulously. 'Don't you know that?'

'I think I only understood it yesterday, when I held you in my arms,' he said gravely. 'I knew you weren't a woman who could make love so passionately, unless...unless...' He swept her up in his arms. 'God, Cordelia, just talking about it sets me on fire!' he exclaimed. 'Let's go back to bed right now!'

'Put me down!' she begged breathlessly, but he was already halfway up the stairs. Somehow they made it to her bedroom, and kicking the door firmly shut behind them, Gil set her down on the bed, pinning her down with his hands and with the eagerly awaited weight of his body. There was no more fight in her then, she returned his kisses fiercely, responding to him until at last they lay spent and triumphant, side by side.

'Now,' he said, still breathing quickly, raising himself on one elbow and looking down on her with fierce male pride of possession, 'we shall have to have the wedding at Mornington, naturally—but we must go to La Vega and celebrate our...er...engagement there. They'll insist on having a *fiesta*, no doubt, and the entire village will stop work for at least three days.'

'Wedding?' Cordelia tried to sit up, but he would not allow her to. 'But, Gil, I thought you were going to marry Alyssa!'

He gave a snort of loud, outraged laughter.

'Do me a favour! I wouldn't touch Alyssa if she and I were the last couple alive on a desert island!' he exclaimed grimly. 'As a matter of fact, she went to Paris two days before we left for Spain. I told her I'd cut her allowance unless she found something useful to do, so she stalked off in a huff, muttering something about modelling. Really, Cordelia, how could you have thought up such nonsense?'

'But she said...and Gaynor thought...' she began weakly.

'When we're married, my love, I hope you'll ask *me* anything you want me to tell you, rather than my sister, or my dimwit cousin,' said Gil, mock-sternly.

She sighed. 'It's a heavenly prospect! Oh, Gil—but you can't marry me!' she said regretfully. 'You're Lord de Mornington, and you need someone who's...well, you know...'

'Who's beautiful? Who's talented?' he queried teasingly. 'Who's as stubborn as they come? It's the 1990s, my darling, and you have all the qualities I need, all that Mornington Hall needs. I love the place, and I fully intend to discharge all my responsibilities towards it,' he went on seriously. 'It's a duty I'll undertake willingly. But I want to involve Ran more in the day-to-day running. Gaynor, too, when she's a business whiz-kid, because every summer I want to be free to spend some time here, in Spain—with you. I don't want any or all of it without you, Cordelia. Understood?'

'Yes, milord!' she said sagely, blue eyes beginning to twinkle wickedly. 'Whatever say! Oh, dear, I have the most dreadful feeling you're going to be the most demanding husband!'

'On that score you need have no doubts, *querida*,' said Gil, pulling her back into his arms. 'No doubts at all!'

4 FREE

Romances and 2 FREE gifts just for you!

*You can enjoy all the
heartwarming emotion of true love for FREE!
Discover the heartbreak and the happiness, the emotion
and the tenderness of the modern relationships in
Mills & Boon Romances.*

*We'll send you 4 captivating Romances as a special offer
from Mills & Boon Reader Service, along with the chance to
have 6 Romances delivered to your door each month.*

Claim your FREE books and gifts overleaf...

An irresistible offer from Mills & Boon

Here's a personal invitation from Mills & Boon Reader Service, to become a regular reader of Romances. To welcome you, we'd like you to have 4 books, a CUDDLY TEDDY and a special MYSTERY GIFT absolutely FREE.

Then you could look forward each month to receiving 6 brand new Romances, delivered to your door, postage and packing free! Plus our free newsletter featuring author news, competitions, special offers and much more.

This invitation comes with no strings attached. You may cancel or suspend your subscription at any time, and still keep your free books and gifts.

It's so easy. Send no money now. Simply fill in the coupon below and post it to -

Reader Service, FREEPOST, PO Box 236, Croydon, Surrey CR9 9EL.

--- NO STAMP REQUIRED ---

Free Books Coupon

Yes! Please rush me my 4 free Romances and 2 free gifts! Please also reserve me a Reader Service subscription. If I decide to subscribe I can look forward to receiving 6 brand new Romances each month for just £9.60, postage and packing free. If I choose not to subscribe I shall write to you within 10 days - I can keep the books and gifts whatever I decide. I may cancel or suspend my subscription at any time. I am over 18 years of age.

Name Mrs/Miss/Ms/Mr _____ EP18R

Address _____

_____

Postcode_____ Signature _____